a gentleman's regret

A PRIDE AND PREJUDICE VARIATION

SARAH WALLACE

darcy

THOUGH HE HAD RIDDEN over the gentle hills and lush forests of Pemberley more than a thousand times, there was not a single day that Fitzwilliam Darcy did not take a moment to look over the vast estate with a sense of wonder and gratitude. Rather than being imposed upon the landscape, the grand house was a compliment to it. He had often heard it compared to his aunt's estate at Rosings Park—especially when he visited Lady Catherine at her home in Kent—but he could not see the similarity with his own eyes. While Pemberly was embraced by the natural beauty of the countryside, Rosings Park perched like a predator above its sprawling estate. They could not have been more different, and he was firm on that.

His gelding whickered eagerly and Darcy smiled as he set his heels into the stirrups and urged his mount into a gallop.

Here, on his estate, away from the rush and noise of the city, he was free.

There were, of course, matters that should captivate his attention more than this morning ride—but they could wait.

Besides, he was heading down to the tenant farms to speak with the menfolk about the effects of a recent rainstorm.

Eventually.

The wind whipped through Darcy's hair as he rode and the rhythmic pound of his horse's hooves against the earth filled his ears. He reveled in the sensation of speed and the way the gelding responded to his every movement. For a moment, he could forget about the endless social obligations and business matters that awaited him back at the house. Out here, it was just him, his steed, and the glorious expanse of nature.

He did not shirk those duties or responsibilities—but he often wished that he could forget them for a time.

There had to be more to life than... duty.

As he crested a hill, he slowed his horse to a trot, and took a deep breath as he looked out over the verdant fields stretching out before him. The winter had been hard, but the snows had melted and given way to the warmer breezes of spring, though a chill still clung to the early morning air. From this distance, he could see the tenant farms, their thatched roofs burnished by the morning sun. He knew he should head there directly, but the temptation to prolong his ride was strong.

Just a bit further.

He urged his horse forward once more and followed the path as it wound through a copse of trees. The dappled sunlight played across his face, and he closed his eyes for a moment, savoring the peace of the moment.

Darcy slowed his horse to a trot to better appreciate the tranquil beauty of his surroundings. He had always found solace in the untamed wilderness of Pemberley—and he preferred them to the stuffy ballrooms and crowded streets of London.

He leaned forward to stroke his horse's neck. "A pity Georgiana doesn't like the outdoors," he said aloud.

The horse snorted in response and Darcy chuckled.

"Quite right. Ballrooms and seasides are where young ladies

play—it is not for the likes of us." He paused and sat up a little straighter. "Well— not for the likes of me," he muttered.

Charles Bingley was better suited to such places. He recalled with some chagrin his last attempt at social interaction... it was better for him to stay at Pemberley, immersed in the business of the estate.

The business of the estate—he could put that off no longer.

As he emerged from the grove, he turned his horse toward the trail that led down through the fields to the rear of the estate. As he approached, Darcy felt a sense of responsibility wash over him. These were his people, and it was his duty to ensure their well-being. He knew that the recent rainstorm, as well as the melting of the winter snow, had swelled the river that ran through the estate and had likely caused damage to their crops and homes, and he was determined to offer whatever assistance he could.

He would speak with the farmers, assess the situation, and do whatever was necessary to help them recover from the storm.

As Darcy approached the tenant farms, he could see the extent of the damage caused by the recent rainstorm. Fields were waterlogged, with tender young shoots of wheat and barley beaten down into the mud. Fences had been washed away, and debris littered the landscape. He could see a group of men gathered near one of the farmhouses and his chest tightened as he saw how grim their faces were as they surveyed the destruction.

Darcy dismounted and handed the reins of his horse to a sturdy lad who had run up to greet him. He strode toward the group of farmers, his boots squelching in the muddy ground. As he drew near, the men turned to face him—relieved that he had come.

"Mr. Darcy," said one of the older men, stepping forward

and touching his cap respectfully. "We're glad to see you, sir. It's been a hard few days, and no mistake."

Darcy nodded as he looked over the damage. "I can see that, Mr. Wilkins. Tell me, how bad is it? What do you need?"

The men exchanged glances, and then Mr. Wilkins spoke again. "The fields are a mess, sir. We'll have to replant most of the crops. And some of the houses have taken damage—roofs leaking, walls crumbling. It'll take weeks to set right."

Darcy listened intently, his brow furrowed. He knew that time was of the essence—the farmers would need to replant their crops as soon as possible to salvage what they could of the growing season. And the damaged homes would, of course, need to be repaired quickly to shelter the families from the elements.

"I will ensure you have the resources and labor you need to recover from this," Darcy said firmly as he met the eyes of each man. "Extra hands will be sent from the house staff to assist in rebuilding. And I will personally see to it that you receive an advance on your rents, as well as seed and supplies, to replant your fields."

The men murmured their thanks and Darcy clasped Mr. Wilkins on the shoulder reassuringly.

"You have always been loyal tenants and served Pemberley well. It is only right that I support you now in your time of need. We will get through this together."

He spent the next hour walking the fields with the farmers to survey the extent of the flooding and discuss recovery plans. By the time he mounted his horse to return to the house, the sun was high in the sky.

As Darcy rode, his mind was preoccupied as he worked through the logistics of coordinating the relief efforts. He would need to review the accounts, and perhaps reallocate some of the discretionary funds.

The planting would have to be expedited—

There was much to do.

Realizing that he had neglected to speak with Mrs. Reynolds, Darcy brought his gelding back to the stables and handed the reins into the capable hands of Pemberley's head groom. "Brush him down well," Darcy called out. "It has been a long morning—"

"I can see that from the mud, sir," the groom laughed and Darcy looked down at his boots.

He cursed under his breath. "Ah, yes," he said wryly. The thick black mud was good for the crops, but Mrs. Reynolds would scold him bitterly if he tracked it into the house.

"Shall I have him ready for an evening ride before the supper bell?" the groom asked.

Darcy dearly wished he could—but there were other duties he had let fall by the wayside.

"I am afraid not," he replied. "But tomorrow morning—I shall not miss it."

"Aye, sir," the groom replied. "He'll be ready."

Darcy thanked the man and strode up the hill toward the house.

He cast an eye over the orchard and gritted his teeth as he remembered that he had not yet spoken with the head gardener about plans for the coming year. There was simply... too much to manage. Too much for one man.

Georgiana would tease him that he needed a wife to look after such things—or at least to take some of the burden from his shoulders. But he would not hear of it.

Pemberley was *his* responsibility.

And his alone.

His stomach rumbled and Darcy took the path that would lead him to Pemberley's kitchens.

Upon entering, he was greeted by the familiar warmth of

the bread ovens and the enticing aromas of various dishes being prepared for the day. He knew each and every servant by name, and the cook, Monsieur Lilet, greeted him with a small bow.

"Good morning, all," Darcy exclaimed. "Have— have you seen Mrs. Reynolds yet this morning?"

"Of course," the cook replied. "She has just been—"

As if on cue, Mrs. Reynolds, swept into the room with an air of authority that only years of experience could bestow.

"Ah, Mr. Darcy," she said. "I was just about to send someone to find you. We need to discuss the menu for this evening."

"Of course," Darcy replied, "shall we walk?"

The housekeeper inclined her head and followed Darcy out of the kitchen and into the corridor.

She paused for just a moment and Darcy froze in place.

"What?"

"Your boots, sir," Mrs. Reynolds replied tersely. "I see you have been in the fields—"

Darcy grimaced. "Indeed I have. Shall I go around?"

Mrs. Reynolds' smile was tight, but amusement sparkled in her dark eyes. "If you please, sir. I know you insist upon traipsing through the mud with the tenants, but you cannot bring it into the house!"

"Quiet right," Darcy said. "I shall meet you in the foyer—"

Mrs. Reynolds continued up the stairs and Darcy turned back to the kitchen. On his way, he snatched a bread roll from one of the baskets and an apple tart before he stepped out of the kitchen and back into the herb garden. Mrs. Reynolds was right, his boots *were* filthy.

As he walked through the garden toward the courtyard, Darcy made a detour toward the creek that rushed by the front of the house. Silver-sided trout leapt in the clear water and Darcy smiled as he counted the flashing shapes. The gamekeeper had outdone himself this year, and the creek was well stocked for spring.

"Excellent," he muttered.

As he turned back to the house, he noticed a carriage approaching.

He wasn't expecting any guests—and had not received any letters announcing any intentions of a visit from his relations or friends...

"What can this be—" he mused aloud.

He waited in the courtyard, hands upon his hips as the carriage rumbled down the road and slowed as it came onto the gravel.

Two trunks were secured to the top of the carriage, and he could only assume that the occupant meant to stay for quite some time.

Even before the carriage came to a stop, the door was flung wide and the familiar figure of Charles Bingley leapt from the confines of the vehicle.

"Charles!" Darcy cried out. "What in heaven's name—"

Charles's expression broke into a wide grin that reached his eyes, revealing the genuine happiness he felt at seeing his dear friend.

"What a pleasant surprise," Darcy exclaimed, extending his hand in a warm greeting. "I had not expected you!"

"Nor did I plan to arrive so suddenly," Charles chuckled as he shook Darcy's hand. "But I have news I simply could not wait to share with you in person."

"Ah, then let us retire to the drawing room and discuss this news over a glass of brandy," Darcy suggested.

"You are covered in mud," Bingley observed.

Darcy looked down at his boots. "So I have been told," he said. "If I bring them into the house Mrs. Reynolds will take my head for it—"

"Good Lord, we do not want that," Charles laughed. "She is a fine housekeeper, but I have been terrified of her for years and I do not mind her knowing it!"

Darcy led Charles around to the side entrance, where he could slip inside and change his muddy boots without incurring Mrs. Reynolds' wrath. After quickly freshening up, he rejoined his friend in the drawing room, where a servant had already poured two glasses of brandy.

"Now then," Darcy said as he settled into an armchair across from Charles, "what is this news that brought you all the way to Pemberley? I had thought you were well seated in... Hertfordshire, was it?"

"Indeed," Charles exclaimed. "I have become quite enamored with my new country home! Netherfield Park is, of course, nothing to Pemberly—but I can see why you are such a country minded sort of man. The fresh air, the rolling hills, the quaint society—it has done wonders for my spirits."

"The country has that power," Darcy said with a smile. "I am glad to hear it suits you so well, Charles. But you did not come all the way to Deryshire to gloat about the country air..."

"No, indeed," Charles continued with some excitement. "I have... I have met someone, Darcy."

"Oh?"

Darcy had not expected that. Bingley's sisters had been trying for *years* to find someone their brother would be even remotely interested in marrying, and all their efforts had yielded nothing. Perhaps it was because they did not understand their brother as well as they believed they did. Darcy had a feeling that every young lady they would bring before Charles would have much in common with *them*, and less in common with Charles than might be required of a bride.

An unfortunate situation when the matchmakers were

concerned with the quality of their own society rather than the happiness of the couple.

Charles did not wait for Darcy to ask any questions and continued with haste. "She is a country gentleman's daughter," he said in a rush. "A young lady named Jane Bennet—I say to you, Darcy, I have never seen a more beautiful creature in all my life! She is kind, generous—such a gentle spirit!"

"But that is wonderful," Darcy said. He had often heard Charles speak kindly of young ladies of his acquaintance, but not with the same vehemence in which he spoke of Miss Jane Bennet.

"I— I could not write to tell you," Bingly said. "I was certain of it the moment I laid eyes upon her, and even more certain once we had danced at the Meryton Assembly—"

Darcy took a sip of his brandy. "Certain of what?"

Bingley's forehead creased slightly. "That she was destined to be my wife," he exclaimed.

Darcy blinked at his friend in surprise. "What?"

"I am to be married," Charles cried.

Darcy was silent for a moment longer than he knew he should be, and Charles' eyes narrowed.

"Did you hear me?" he asked.

"Yes, of course," Darcy sputtered. "Forgive me, my friend. It is indeed most wonderful news!" He rose to shake Bingley's hand. "I am truly happy for you. Miss Bennet must be a remarkable young lady to have captured your heart so."

"Thank you," Charles replied sincerely and Darcy noted how his friend's neck flushed red with delight as he spoke. "She is, indeed, extraordinary, and I cannot wait for you to meet her. And to see what I have done with Netherfield Park—Caroline would not permit me to keep it if I did not redecorate, and I have done my best to please her— Also, Darcy, if I may— I would be honored if you could stand beside me on my wedding day."

"Of course, Charles," Darcy answered without hesitation. "I would be honored. And you are welcome to stay at Pemberley for as long as you wish." He glanced at the clock on the mantel and drained the last of his brandy before setting the glass down. "But let us finish this conversation at dinner. If we are not seated promptly at seven, Mrs. Reynolds will never let me hear the end of it. Your trunks should be in your usual room by now—"

"Of course," Charles replied but his expression shifted to one of mild panic as he imagined Mrs. Reynolds' threatened scolding. He drank the remainder of his bourbon in one gulp and grimaced. "I shall see you at the dining table," he choked out.

Darcy bid his friend farewell and made his way through the grand halls of Pemberley toward his bedchamber. As he walked, Darcy couldn't help but dwell on the news of Charles' engagement.

Charles was impulsive—he had always been an unserious sort of gentleman, but his sincerity made up for it. Darcy was, of course, concerned that his friend had not considered all of his options and had been drawn in by a pretty face...

What were her relations like? And the society she kept?

What was her father's income?

All important questions that should have been considered before any proposal was made—and now it was, surely, too late to refuse or change his mind...

No, it was a ridiculous notion.

Charles was a grown man—and heir to a fortune. He had been the head of his household for the better part of the last decade, what right did Darcy have not to trust his judgement?

Still, the prospect of love and companionship stirred a

longing deep within him that he had not allowed himself to acknowledge in quite some time.

His own reluctance to allow himself to entertain such things.

The young ladies who had been paraded before him in the past had all been approved by his aunt—and none of them had been interesting in the slightest. They were all, of course, accomplished young women from good families with a sizable income... but they had not been right for him.

That Charles had been able to find a young lady suited to him in such a...

No. He could not think on it.

Such a thing was impossible for him.

Upon reaching his room, he closed the door behind him and crossed the room to the washbasin. The jug of water on the marble tabletop would be chilled now, but that did not matter.

He stared at his reflection in the looking glass and took note of the faint lines that had begun to appear around his eyes. It was not too late to take a wife... he knew far too many older gentlemen who were quite happily in pursuit of their second and third wives. His own father had married for the second time quite late in life and he had been happy.

He chuckled at his own foolish thoughts. He was not so old yet.

Plenty of time to find a bride and have a family.

God willing.

Or... perhaps it would be easier to pretend that such things did not concern him.

The estate was more than enough to manage.

And if he had no children, Georgiana would inherit everything.

He could not be displeased with that.

Darcy poured water into the washbasin and splashed it

onto his face. He allowed the droplets to slide down his cheeks, momentarily refreshing him from his contemplative thoughts.

He dried his face with a soft piece of linen and proceeded to choose his attire for dinner.

He chose an elegant waistcoat of deep green, accompanied by a fine linen shirt and a fawn colored neck cloth that matched his trousers. As he fastened the buttons and adjusted his attire, Darcy's mind wandered back to the conversation he'd had with Charles.

Charles had always been in search of the finer things in life —and with them, the accomplishments that marked the passage of time. A country estate, a house in town, and now... a wife. And, soon enough, children to fill both houses at Christmastide.

Next he would acquire a flock of hunting dogs and become an insufferable gentleman like all the others.

Darcy shook his head.

Despite the longing he felt, he knew he could not deny the contentment that accompanied his quiet life at Pemberley.

As he took one final glance at his reflection, Fitzwilliam Darcy allowed himself a small, satisfied smile.

He was grateful for the life he had built and the tranquility it offered.

Having a wife and children would only complicate things.

He could not see any point in changing what was, as far as he could tell, everything was perfectly suited to him.

TWO

darcy

IN THE DEAD OF NIGHT, Fitzwilliam Darcy sat up in bed.

An unexpected storm roared outside and its howling winds shook the windows. His first thought was for the tenant farmers—they had already been through too much hardship with the violent weather that had battered the countryside over the last weeks.

He slid out of bed and dressed quickly—if he needed to take a horse down to the tenant farms, he would be prepared.

Rain pelted the windows and hammered against the roof as he lit a candle and hurried out of the room and made his way downstairs.

Darcy's mind was filled with concern for the safety of Pemberley, as some of the windows and doors had a tendency to leak during storms of this nature.

He wandered through the first floor of the manor to ensure all the doors were closed and secure.

However, when he passed by the foyer he took a few steps toward the front door to test the lock, and as he paused, a strange sound just outside caught his attention.

At first, he thought it was one of the barn cats seeking shelter from the rain, but they usually came to the kitchen door for scraps and affection—not the front door.

As he listened more intently, he realized this was no feline cry.

Curiosity piqued, Darcy cautiously unlocked and opened the heavy front door.

A cold wind rushed in and sniffed out the candle's flame.

"Damn," he muttered.

He peered out into the stormy night but saw nothing through the driving rain. Darcy was about to close the door when he heard the sound again—louder this time.

At first, it looked like little more than a parcel left in the rain.

But after a moment of letting his eyes adjust, Darcy realized in horror that the package was a baby.

Nestled in a small basket, the infant was wrapped securely in a woolen blanket.

Rain pelted the small form, and Darcy felt a sudden surge of protectiveness for the vulnerable child.

"Good heavens," he muttered as he set the candle down and bent to scoop the basket up off the steps and brought it indoors. He kicked the door closed behind him and shouted for Mrs. Reynolds.

The child, alarmed by the sudden change in circumstance, let out a faint cry.

"Hush now," he said. "You are safe."

He called out urgently for Mrs. Reynolds again and heard footsteps on the landing above him as Bingley emerged from his room. He looked disheveled and alarmed as he rushed down the stairs.

"What the devil is the matter?" Bingley asked. "I heard

shouting—and the storm—" He paused as his eyes landed on the basket in Darcy's arms. "What— What is that?"

Mrs. Reynolds, somewhat disheveled, but otherwise her usual prim self, arrived carrying a lamp.

"Whatever is the matter?" she asked. Her eyes were wide with concern. "I heard shouting—"

"It seems we have another visitor," Darcy said.

Both Mrs. Reynolds and Bingley stared down the infant, their faces a mask of frozen shock.

"Who in the world is that?" Bingley muttered.

"I have not the slightest idea," Darcy replied, his brow furrowed in confusion. "I do not even have any friends with children. But I opened the door and found it there in the rain—" He paused to set the basket down and lifted the infant out and settled it into his arms.

Who could have left this child on his doorstep? And why?

Surely there were better places to leave a child than the doorstep of a stranger.

"Did you see anyone?" Bingley asked.

"I did not hear any knocking," Mrs. Reynolds offered. "I shall ask the maids—"

"I did not see anyone nearby," Darcy said, "but given the danger to the child, I did not linger to look. It seemed more important to get it out of the rain."

Mrs. Reynolds, ever the motherly figure, passed the lantern to Bingley, gently took the baby from Darcy's arms, and held it against her chest as though it were her own grandchild.

Now holding the lantern, Bingley's focus was distracted by the basket the child had arrived in.

"Here now," he said. He crouched down, reached into the basket, and drew something out. "There appears to be a message."

He held out a small, unevenly folded piece of paper. Unsealed.

Darcy took the note with cautious fingers and opened it.

"Dear Fitzwilliam," Darcy read aloud. "This child is a Darcy, and she needs your love and protection. Please care for her as if she is your own. Her name is Amelia."

He paused and the words hung in the air, leaving them all momentarily speechless.

"Amelia," Mrs. Reynolds repeated softly as she looked down at the infant with a tender smile upon her face. "That is a lovely name."

The lantern light cast shadows on the walls as Darcy and Charles exchanged troubled glances.

The rain continued to pound against the windows and the wind moaned in the corners. An inauspicious night. The clock struck midnight and Darcy frowned at the note in his hand.

"Is it signed?" Charles asked.

Darcy shook his head, eyes still glued to the parchment. "No, not a word to indicate who might have left her here. And I do not recognize the handwriting."

"Curious indeed," Charles mused as he rubbed his chin thoughtfully. He glanced over at Mrs. Reynolds, who was tenderly holding the small baby in her arms. A worried expression twisted across her face.

With a sigh, Darcy carefully re-folded the note and pushed it into the pocket of his trousers. He bent to retrieve the basket, and as he did so, he noticed a small object tucked under the edge of the blanket. Reaching in, he retrieved a delicate doll made of worn and faded fabric. He studied the simple toy, in the hope that it might offer some clue as to the child's origins, but found none.

A flicker of concern crossed Mrs. Reynolds' face as she

cradled the infant in her arms. "Mr. Darcy— What do you intend to do?"

Darcy hesitated. He wasn't certain—not at all.

Responsibility for the child's well-being reared up inside him and he considered the possibility that whoever had left the child on his doorstep had hoped he would feel such a stirring. He did not like being manipulated, yet he was at a loss as to what course of action to take.

"I have no idea, Mrs. Reynolds," he admitted quietly. "But whatever is to be done, it will not happen tonight."

"Perhaps it would be best if I retire for the evening then," Charles suggested. "But if you find you need my assistance, do not hesitate to shout my name in the dead of night, to terrify me from sleep once again."

"I shall do so," Darcy chuckled. "However, I shall see to it that everything is taken care of. Rest well, Bingley."

Charles brushed a hand through his wild golden curls, handed the lantern to Darcy, and executed a mock bow toward himself and Mrs. Reynolds. "Goodnight then."

With a final glance at the mysterious child, Charles retreated to his chamber, leaving Darcy and Mrs. Reynolds alone in the dimly lit foyer.

"Mrs. Reynolds," Darcy began, "I will retrieve Georgiana's old bassinet from the attic. In the meantime—"

"I do not think you are the one to instruct me on how to care for a child," Mrs. Reynolds admonished with a smile. "I shall take her to the kitchens. She will be very well looked after."

Relief flooded through his chest. "You are... I know she will be safe in your hands," he said.

"And, sir, if you don't mind, I will question the other maids and footmen to see if they know of anyone who might have left the child here— There is a chance they might have seen someone skulking around. This is not a deed that is done lightly —or without planning."

Darcy sighed, his heart heavy with the sudden burden thrust upon him. "You are quite correct," he said. "I shall hope that we might find the child's mother before long."

"As do I," Mrs. Reynolds said. "She is very young— I do believe one of the scullery maids just had a child. She might be able to nurse her— But I will not bore you with such things," she said in a rush. "The child will be well cared for, you have my promise of that."

"Thank you," Darcy said sincerely.

"Now, sir, please go back to bed. The house is secure, and the child is with me. There is nothing else to concern you this night."

Darcy nodded. Thus dismissed, he handed the lantern back to Mrs. Reynolds, retrieved his candle and returned to the second floor and his bedchamber.

So much for the peace and quiet of Pemberley, he thought wistfully.

The sound of rain pattering against the windows accompanied him as he ascended the grand staircase, and each step he took echoed through the empty halls.

Charles Bingley's snores were muffled by the heavy door of his chamber and Darcy chuckled as he passed.

The note in his pocket was heavy and he repeated its words in his mind.

She is a Darcy.

He had no idea who delivered this baby into his life, but he certainly was not going to abandon her to some orphanage— especially if she were a Darcy.

No; he would find a way to sort all of this out...

Somehow.

THREE

darcy

THE SILENCE of the drawing room, in which Darcy usually enjoyed his morning coffee and a few hours of reading, was now filled with conversation as Mrs. Reynolds gave her report of everything the infant had done and been given over the course of the night.

The storm had abated somewhat, and Darcy sat in a plush armchair with baby Amelia cradled gently in his arms. His coffee was forgotten on the side table while Darcy was focused on the infant and the way her tiny fingers grasped at the air.

He studied her delicate features, trying to find some semblance of familiarity in them.

"Do you see any— does she look like anyone you might know, Mrs. Reynolds?" Darcy asked finally.

The housekeeper shook her head. "I am afraid not, sir." She took a breath, "I did ask the maids if they might know anyone who had a child recently— or if they had heard any gossip in Lambton, but they knew nothing—at least, nothing they would say to me. The footmen have reported nothing out of the ordinary and no strangers have been on the property..."

Bingley, who had been pacing the room, hesitated before speaking.

"I hate to bring it up, Darcy..." he began. "And I am sure it is impossible." He paused again and Darcy's irritation rose just a little. "However, could it perhaps be possible that..." he trailed off.

"Spit it out, man," Darcy said shortly.

"Could she be... Georgiana's child?" Bingley asked tentatively.

Indignation flared in Darcy's chest, but it faded just as quickly. He knew there was no malice in his friend's question.

"It is not possible," Darcy replied evenly. "I saw my sister at Ramsgate only a few months past—there would have been no way to keep this particular secret."

As if sensing the tension in the arms that held her, Amelia's peaceful expression twisted into one of discomfort, and soon, she began to cry. Her wails echoed throughout the drawing room and tugged at Darcy's heartstrings. He held her close and attempted to soothe her, but to no avail.

Mrs. Reynolds approached with a soothing smile upon her face.

"Do not look so terrified, sir," she said as she took the child from Darcy's arms. "She needs to eat, and that is not your responsibility," she stated firmly. "However, I must tell you that if you do plan to keep her here at Pemberley, she will need a caretaker—a nurse."

As much as he hated to admit it, Mrs. Reynolds was quite correct. The child had been in the house for less than two days and everything seemed to be in disarray. "But who might we engage for such a task? Should we send inquiries into Lambton? Or London?"

"On short notice, as well—" Bingley mused. "Louisa was complaining of a friend of hers in London who had to engage a nurse the moment she discovered she was pregnant." He tugged at his jacket and frowned. "Who can think of planning so far ahead for such a thing? A damned hassle if you ask me."

Mrs. Reynolds' expression was tight. "Indeed, sir, we need someone trustworthy. Not only someone who will care for Miss Amelia as if she were their own., but also someone that we can trust in this house."

Another aspect he had not considered.

His jaw tightened. "Agreed," Darcy murmured, his gaze once again focused on the tiny child in the housekeeper's arms. "But where do we find such a person?"

Darcy knew that time was of the essence, but the solution seemed to be slipping further from his grasp.

Suddenly, Bingley's expression brightened. "I have it," he cried.

Darcy looked at him in surprise and the child fussed in Mrs. Reynolds' arms.

"Well? What is it?" Darcy asked. It was difficult to keep the irritation from his voice, but Charles did not seem to notice.

"Perhaps my fiancé's sister, Miss Elizabeth Bennet, might be suited in the role," Bingley suggested. "She has a genuine warmth and kindness about her that would make her an excellent nurse—and if the child liked her, she could stay on as her governess."

"Indeed—if she is suitable then that would be a most agreeable arrangement," Darcy replied. "You must tell me more of her, Charles. Is she accomplished?"

"Well," Bingley began. "She is not so accomplished as your dear sister—but I believe very few young women could be."

Darcy did not like his friend's tone.

"But, Miss Bennet is a remarkable young woman," Bingley continued in a rush. "She possesses a lively wit and is forever reading— She is spirited on the dance floor, and my dear Jane tells me that she loves to laugh— In my estimation, she is... a joyful young woman, and I have never known her to be cross or ill-tempered."

Darcy pondered the information for a moment. "Do you think she would be amenable to such an arrangement?"

"I cannot say for certain, but it is worth considering," Bingley replied. "I shall write to my dear Jane and inquire about Miss Elizabeth's interest in the position."

"Very well, Charles. Please do so," Darcy said. "She will, of course, be paid—as would be expected. I do not wish to insult her or take her away from other commitments—but I am in a peculiar position."

"I shall make that clear," Charles said with a smile.

Satisfied for the moment, Mrs. Reynolds swept out of the room with the child. Bingley also left the room to pen his letter, and Darcy was left to marvel at the rapid turn his life had taken.

* * *

DARCY WAITED for weeks for Charles to bring him a reply to his letter.

He told himself that he was not nervous—how could he be?

But he was on edge, that much was certain.

The child was being cared for in the kitchens when it was time for her to be fed, but the remainder of her time was spent in a bassinet beside the desk in his study while he worked, or beside his chair in the drawing room while he read.

Wherever he was, little Amelia was not far away.

And after a few days, Darcy had trouble remembering what it was like to be alone in the big house.

She reminded him of Georgiana when she had first been born. Quiet and sweet. Sleeping and cooing. But she was not Georgiana's child. It was impossible. Her letters were uncomplicated and happy as they always were, and she seemed genuinely surprised when he made mention of the child's arrival.

The only time he left her in Mrs. Reynolds' care was when he ventured down to the tenant farms to assist with their rebuilding.

He immersed himself in work on the estate to keep from dwelling upon the possibility that another new face would be coming to Pemberley.

As the days passed, Darcy found himself growing more attached to little Amelia. Her presence brought a new light into the halls of Pemberley, and he couldn't help but smile every time he heard her soft coos and gurgles. Mrs. Reynolds doted on the child as if she were her own granddaughter, ensuring that she was well-fed, clean, and content.

But so many questions remained—where had the child come from? And whose child *was* she? Darcy could see no resemblance to any of his family members in her tiny face, but he supposed that was common with infants.

Perhaps in time—

One evening, as Darcy sat in his study with Amelia nestled in the crook of his arm, a gentle knock at the door interrupted his thoughts. "Come in," he called out as he carefully adjusted the baby's position.

Charles Bingley entered, a broad grin spread across his face. "I have wonderful news, Darcy," he announced. He brandished a letter like a victory flag. "Miss Elizabeth Bennet has accepted the position as Amelia's nurse and governess. She will be arriving at Pemberley with my dear Jane within a fortnight."

Darcy felt a wave of relief wash over him. "That is wonderful news indeed, Charles. And I look forward to meeting your intended bride as well"

Bingley chuckled. "I must admit, I am quite eager to see

how Miss Elizabeth will fare in this role. If she is anything like her elder sister, which I know her to be, I have no doubt that she will be an excellent caretaker for little Amelia."

Darcy nodded, his gaze returning to the sleeping infant in his arms. "I am grateful for her willingness to take on this responsibility. It will be a relief to have someone dedicated to Amelia's care and education."

Bingley's expression softened as he observed his friend cradling the baby with such tenderness. "You seem to have grown quite fond of her, Darcy."

A small smile tugged at the corners of Darcy's mouth. "I cannot deny it. She has brought an unexpected joy to Pemberley. But I know that I cannot provide her with the nurturing and attention she requires on my own. Miss Bennet's arrival will be most welcome."

"Indeed," Bingley agreed. "And I have no doubt that you will come to appreciate Miss Elizabeth's presence as well. She is a remarkable young woman, Darcy. Full of life and spirit."

Darcy raised an eyebrow. "Is that so? Well, I shall look forward to making her acquaintance and seeing for myself."

As the two men continued to discuss the impending arrival of the Bennet sisters, Amelia stirred in Darcy's arms, her tiny eyelids fluttering open. Darcy gently rocked her, and his deep voice soothed her back to slumber.

The next fortnight passed in a flurry of preparations. Mrs. Reynolds busied herself readying a suite of rooms for Miss Elizabeth Bennet that would include Amelia's cradle and all of her blankets and clothing which had been acquired in a very short amount of time.

The day of Miss Elizabeth Bennet's arrival at Pemberley dawned bright and clear. Darcy found himself pacing the length of his study, Amelia cradled securely in his arms as he awaited the arrival of their new governess.

Though he trusted Bingley's judgement implicitly, Darcy could not help but feel a twinge of apprehension. Inviting a stranger into his home, and entrusting her with the care of this precious child who had so unexpectedly become his charge—it was no small matter.

A knock at the door interrupted his musings. "Come in," Darcy called out, turning to face the entrance.

Mrs. Reynolds entered, a smile upon her face. "Mr. Darcy, the carriage has been spotted coming up the drive. Miss Bennet and her sister shall be arriving presently."

Darcy nodded, taking a deep breath to steady himself. "Very good, Mrs. Reynolds. Please ensure that all is in readiness for their arrival. I shall greet them in the foyer."

"Of course, sir," Mrs. Reynolds replied with a small curtsy before hurrying off to make the final preparations.

Darcy glanced down at Amelia, who was beginning to stir in his arms. "Well, little one," he murmured softly, "it seems your new governess has arrived. Let us hope she is all that Bingley promises."

With Amelia securely nestled in his arms, Darcy made his way down the grand staircase to the foyer just as the front doors were opened by the footmen. Bingley practically bounded in, his face alight with excitement and joy. Following close behind him were two young ladies, both lovely in their own distinct ways.

The first, who Darcy presumed to be Miss Jane Bennet based on Bingley's effusive descriptions, was a true beauty with golden hair, delicate features, and a serene smile that seemed to radiate warmth and kindness. But it was the second young lady who caught and held Darcy's attention.

Miss Elizabeth Bennet was not a classic beauty like her sister, but there was something undeniably captivating about her. Her eyes sparkled with intelligence and curiosity as she looked around the foyer. Her smile, when she turned it upon him, was bright and genuine, and she carried herself with a confident grace.

As the party approached, Darcy found himself standing a bit straighter, suddenly very aware of the sleeping infant in his arms and the responsibility he bore.

"Darcy, my good man!" Bingley greeted him enthusiastically, clasping his hand in a firm shake. "May I present my lovely fiancée, Miss Jane Bennet, and her sister, Miss Elizabeth Bennet."

The ladies curtsied gracefully and Darcy inclined his head in response, mindful not to disturb Amelia. "You are both very welcome to Pemberley."

Miss Jane Bennet smiled warmly. "Thank you for your hospitality, Mr. Darcy. Your home is truly magnificent."

"It is our pleasure to have you here," Darcy replied and then his gaze shifted to Miss Elizabeth. "And Miss Elizabeth, I must extend my sincere gratitude for your willingness to take on the role of governess for little Amelia. It is a great relief to know she will be in capable hands."

Elizabeth's eyes sparkled as she looked at the sleeping child in his arms. "It is an honor, Mr. Darcy. I look forward to getting to know Amelia and helping to guide her as she grows."

Darcy found himself captivated by the melody of her voice and the genuine warmth in her expression. He cleared his throat, realizing he had been staring perhaps a moment too long. "Well then, shall we adjourn to the drawing room? Mrs. Reynolds has prepared refreshments after your journey."

As the group made their way to the drawing room, Darcy found his attention constantly drawn to Elizabeth. She engaged in lively conversation with Bingley and her sister, her quick wit and intelligent observations evident in every word.

Once settled in the drawing room, Darcy carefully transferred Amelia into Elizabeth's waiting arms. As he did so, their hands brushed briefly and sent an unexpected jolt of awareness through him. Elizabeth seemed not to notice, her attention fully focused on the child she now held.

The moment Amelia was in Elizabeth's arms, the baby's fussing ceased, and was replaced by contented cooing. Darcy observed the gentle way in which Elizabeth held her, and the way her hands soothed the infant with ease. In that instant, he knew that she was the perfect person to care for the child.

"Miss Bennet," Darcy began, "your... fitness for this position is already evident, and I have no doubt that you are the right person to care for Amelia. I am grateful to you for agreeing to take on this burden."

"She will not be a burden at all," Elizabeth replied, her eyes never leaving the baby's face. "I am honored by your trust in me and will gladly accept the position, though I must tell you—" She looked up briefly. "I am happy to stay. However, I would ask that you tell me if my presence here is too much of a distraction for you— I do not wish to intrude upon your daily life here—"

"No, indeed," Darcy said quickly. "I am certain that there will be no intrusion at all."

Elizabeth smiled and focused on the child once more as Mrs. Reynolds brought in a tea service with the assistance of another servant. He did not wish for her to second-guess her agreement. Should he have set out a contract? Was she an employee now? There had been no discussion of payment or... anything.

Perhaps those were problems for a later time.

For now, life could go back to some semblance of normality...

darcy

DARCY FROWNED at the light of the early morning sun that streamed through the window of his bedchamber. He had woken early, determined to assist Elizabeth in her adjustment to her duties as Amelia's nurse, as well as answer any questions she might have about her new home. He was not convinced that his services were entirely needed, but he wished to do his best to be a part of the process just the same.

As he descended the grand staircase, Darcy relished the quiet of the house—he was used to his solitude here. Georgiana was so often away with her friends at the seaside... and for a moment he wondered if it was his own stoic nature that had driven her away from her family home.

Thoughts for another time.

Darcy expected to find the parlor empty at this early hour, but as he entered the room he was greeted by the sight of Elizabeth, who was already tending to baby Amelia. The child lay nestled in a bassinet, sleeping peacefully while Elizabeth read a book by the fireside.

"Good morning, Miss Bennet," Darcy said softly so as not to

disturb the child. "I must admit I did not expect to see you awake so early."

Elizabeth closed her book immediately and set it aside as he approached and he felt suddenly self-conscious as her dark eyes appraised him. "Ah, Mr. Darcy," she said and her face lit up with a warm smile. "It seems neither of us are well-acquainted with the habits of infants. Miss Amelia saw to it that I barely slept— But there will be time for my own rest later."

She did not seem cross—entirely the opposite—and her voice was filled with fondness for the tiny child beside her chair.

"I see," he responded. "I thought— I thought it might be a good day to show you the estate... if this is to be your home..."

"Thank you, Mr. Darcy," she said. "It is, indeed, a lovely day for such a distraction. However, Mrs. Reynolds has informed me that she was able to acquire a perambulator and I was just about to take Amelia for a walk around the gardens. If you would like, it would be very helpful to have a guide so we do not lose our way..."

"I believe I would," he agreed, feeling somewhat flustered by her invitation though he did not know why. It was his house, after all. And he had intended to show her the gardens—

Get it together, man.

Charles would have laughed to see him so discomfited.

Elizabeth gathered up Amelia from her bassinet and they walked together to the servery where Mrs. Reynolds had, indeed, kept a very fine wicker perambulator.

With Amelia safely nestled inside, Darcy escorted them out to the gardens and he was pleased to see that the perambulator rolled smoothly over the gravel paths. A thought struck him suddenly that he would never have experienced such a thing in any other circumstance—it was not that he had entirely abandoned the idea of having a family of his own... but the urgency of such a thing had faded somewhat as the affairs of the estate had overtaken his life.

The morning air was crisp and invigorating, and the meticulously maintained flowerbeds and hedges were shown to their best advantage. He could not have asked for a better day.

Or better company.

Darcy found himself thoroughly engaged in conversation with Elizabeth, and her quick wit and insightful observations kept him on his toes. She had a way of seeing the world that was both refreshing and challenging, and he could not help but be drawn to her unique perspective.

As they rounded a bend in the path, Elizabeth paused to admire a particularly beautiful rose bush. "Your gardens are truly magnificent, Mr. Darcy," she remarked, gently touching a delicate pink blossom. "I can see why you take such pride in Pemberley."

Darcy felt a swell of pride at her words. "Thank you, Miss Bennet. It is a labor of love, to be sure. My mother was particularly fond of the roses, and I have endeavored to maintain them in her memory."

Elizabeth's smile was soft. "That is a lovely tribute. I am sure she would be pleased to know how well you have cared for her beloved gardens."

As they continued down the paths, Darcy took pains to point out several details of interest, including the sculptures his father had selected while on a tour of Italy, and the orchard that stretched down toward the stables.

"Tell me, Miss Bennet," Darcy said in a moment of silence. "What was your childhood like at Longbourn? Bingley has told me little about your family."

Elizabeth's expression turned thoughtful at Darcy's question. "Longbourn is a modest estate compared to Pemberley, but it holds a special place in my heart. I grew up surrounded by the love of my parents and sisters, though I will admit, our household could be rather... lively at times, with five daughters under one roof."

She chuckled softly, and Darcy found himself enchanted by the musical sound.

"My father's library was my refuge," Elizabeth continued, her eyes sparkling with fond memories. "I spent countless hours there, lost in the pages of books. My mother, on the other hand, has always been more concerned with securing advantageous marriages for us than with our education." She grimaced slightly. "I had hoped to tell you this at a later time, but I feel that you must know—"

Darcy paused as confusion streaked through him.

Know what?

Was she also engaged to be married and had not said so?

Was her time here limited? Had she changed her mind?

"Do not look so terrified," Elizabeth laughed. In the pram, baby Amelia fussed and Elizabeth reached in to soothe her.

"I am not— What were you saying?" Darcy said and hoped that Elizabeth would not mistake his awkwardness for anger or frustration.

"I merely meant to tell you that I am not as... accomplished as you might wish a young lady to be," she said. Darcy could see self-consciousness in her expression, but did not know what to say to quell it. His own sister was one of the most accomplished young ladies of his acquaintance, and Mr. Bingley's sisters were similarly skilled. How was it that Miss Bennet could not be?

But she had mentioned that her mother had neglected their education—

"I play pianoforte very ill," Elizabeth said in a rush. "Though I am passably good at French and poetry... I am terrible at drawing. My younger sister Kitty is much more talented than I, perhaps when Amelia is old enough we might engage Kitty's assistance..."

Darcy could not help his smile.

Or his relief.

"Do not worry about such things," he said. "My sister Georgiana is very skilled in pianoforte and sings very well, indeed. I am certain that Amelia's accomplishments will not be neglected."

"Oh..."

Darcy worried that he had insulted her, but Elizabeth's expression was composed and she did not say anything more.

As they continued their walk, the scent of the roses filled the air, and the gentle crunch of gravel underfoot provided a comforting rhythm. Darcy noticed Elizabeth's thoughtful expression, and her eyes, which had been taking in the beauty of the gardens, now turned to him with an inquisitive glint.

"Mr. Darcy," she began hesitantly, "may I be so bold as to inquire about Amelia's parentage? Mr. Bingley was somewhat... vague."

Darcy let out a heavy sigh. "I wish I could answer your question properly, Miss Bennet, but the truth is that I know very little, myself. She was left on my doorstep during a storm—"

"Oh, dear," Elizabeth exclaimed.

"A note was left in her basket," he continued. "It asserted that she was a Darcy, but not who the father was..."

"How can you be certain that it was the truth?" Elizabeth asked, her brow furrowing. "Or are you choosing to trust the person who abandoned her in the rain?"

He paused as he considered her words.

"I suppose that I have no choice," he said finally. "All I have is the letter... and nothing more."

"You mentioned your sister," Elizabeth ventured.

"No, indeed," Darcy said somewhat more sharply than he

intended. "Georgiana... She is not Georgiana's child. I feel that I would know it in an instant if she were." He felt his neck growing hot beneath the collar of his shirt. "Besides," he continued. "I have seen not two months ago, and she was certainly not with child—"

"Of course," Elizabeth murmured.

They walked on in silence as Amelia slept, each lost in their thoughts.

"Has a wet nurse been engaged?" Elizabeth asked suddenly.

"I believe so," Darcy replied. "But you shall have to speak to Mrs. Reynolds about that—"

"Indeed," Elizabeth said.

She seemed somewhat embarrassed to have asked such a question, but it was Darcy who felt that he should have known the answer. *Why did such a simple question leave him feeling as though he were neglectful of his new charge?*

As they neared the house, Darcy felt the need to fill the silence once more, but Elizabeth was quicker.

"I shall take Amelia down to the servery for her feeding, but perhaps you could come visit with her after supper?"

"Of course," he replied, eager to spend more time with the child. "But will you not join me for supper?"

"Thank you for the invitation," she said with a smile, "but I must keep to the baby's schedule and eat when she is sleeping. Mrs. Reynolds has been gracious enough to set a place for me at the servants' table. However, I shall see you afterwards."

Darcy was at once disappointed and more than a little irritated that he had not been informed of this change. He had expected to have Elizabeth as a guest at his table—or at the very least that she would take her meals in her own room or the parlor... This was very odd, indeed.

"Very well, Miss Bennet. I look forward to it."

As Elizabeth departed with Amelia, Darcy made his way to

the library. Upon entering, he found Bingley engrossed in a book. He approached his friend, curiosity piquing as he inquired about Jane's whereabouts.

"Charles, where has Miss Bennet gone?"

"Ah, Darcy," Bingley replied, looking up from his reading. "Jane is visiting with her Aunt and Uncle who have come to Lambton for a few days."

"I see," Darcy said softly. His gaze lingered on the bookshelves lining the library walls, his thoughts still occupied with Elizabeth and baby Amelia. He could not help but be impressed by how quickly she had adapted to her role as the child's caregiver.

"Tell me, Darcy," Bingley began, breaking through the silence. "Do you think Miss Elizabeth will be a tolerable companion?"

"Indeed, I do," Darcy responded. "The child is obviously too young to speak for herself, but she seems calm in Miss Bennet's presence—"

Charles laughed. "Darcy, you fool. I mean for *you*. She will be living in this house— Do *you* believe she will be tolerable?"

Darcy found himself at a loss for words, which only made Charles laugh harder.

"Ah—"

Darcy cleared his throat, feeling slightly flustered by Bingley's question. "Miss Elizabeth is a most agreeable companion. Her wit and intelligence make for engaging conversation, and her gentle manner with Amelia is truly admirable. I have no doubt that her presence at Pemberley will be a welcome addition."

Bingley's eyes sparkled with mirth as he observed his friend's discomfort. "I am glad to hear it, Darcy. And I must say, it is quite refreshing to see you so... animated when speaking of a young lady. Perhaps little Amelia is not the only one who will benefit from Miss Elizabeth's presence."

Darcy shot his friend a stern look, but he could not entirely suppress the slight upward twitch of his lips. "Do not be ridiculous, Charles. Miss Elizabeth is here as Amelia's governess, nothing more. It would be entirely inappropriate to suggest otherwise."

Bingley held up his hands in mock surrender, still grinning. "Of course, of course. Far be it from me to imply anything improper. I am merely pleased to see you enjoying some pleasant company, my friend."

Darcy shook his head. "And what of your own pleasant company, Charles? I trust Miss Bennet is enjoying her time with her relatives?"

"Oh, indeed!" Bingley exclaimed, his face lighting up at the mention of his beloved Jane. "She was quite delighted at the prospect of seeing her aunt and uncle. They are very fond of her, and she of them. I believe they plan to take her to the shops in Lambton to select some items for the wedding—though I do believe there will be better selection in London, she would not be dissuaded, and I would not deny her anything she wished for all the world." He let out a contented sigh. "She will return this evening, and I am counting the hours until I can see her lovely face again."

Darcy couldn't help but smile at his friend's obvious joy. "I am happy for you, Charles, truly. Miss Bennet seems a wonderful match for you. I look forward to getting to know her better during her stay at Pemberley."

"Thank you, Darcy," Bingley replied sincerely. "Your approval means a great deal to me. I know Jane is eager to become better acquainted with you as well. But tell me, how was your walk with Miss Elizabeth and little Amelia? The gardens are looking splendid this time of year."

Darcy's expression softened as he recalled the pleasant morning stroll. "The gardens were indeed at their best, and Miss Elizabeth seemed to appreciate their beauty. She has a keen eye and a thoughtful nature. Our conversation was...enlightening."

Bingley leaned forward, his curiosity piqued. "Oh? Do tell, Darcy. What did you discuss?"

Darcy hesitated for a moment, not wishing to betray Elizabeth's confidence. "We spoke of her family and upbringing at Longbourn. It seems her childhood was a happy one, though perhaps not as focused on the typical accomplishments expected of young ladies."

Bingley nodded thoughtfully and then chuckled. "Yes, the Bennet household is *certainly* a lively one."

"She also inquired about Amelia's parentage, which I'm afraid I could not shed much light on beyond the note that was left with her."

"A mystery, to be sure," Bingley mused. "But it seems that you are determined to do right by the child, regardless of her origins."

Darcy's expression grew serious. "Of course I am. She is an innocent in all of this. It is my duty to ensure she is well cared for and raised properly. I am grateful to have Miss Elizabeth's assistance in that endeavor, and your help in bringing her here."

Bingley smiled knowingly. "I am happy to have been of service. And perhaps, in time, you may come to appreciate Miss Elizabeth's presence for reasons beyond her role as Amelia's governess."

Darcy shot his friend a warning look. "Charles, I have already told you—"

"I know, I know," Bingley interrupted, holding up his hands in a placating gesture. "I meant nothing untoward, truly. I simply believe that you and Miss Elizabeth may find you have more in common than just a shared concern for Amelia's well-being. Friendship between a gentleman and young lady is not unheard of, after all."

Darcy considered his friend's words. It was true that he found Elizabeth's company engaging and her perspective refreshing. Perhaps there was no harm in allowing a friendship to develop, so long as propriety was maintained.

"I suppose you may have a point, Charles," Darcy conceded. "Miss Elizabeth is an intelligent and amiable young woman. I see no reason why we cannot enjoy a cordial acquaintance as she fulfills her role as Amelia's governess."

Bingley grinned, clearly pleased with himself. "Splendid! I have a feeling you two will get on famously." He set down his book and stood from his chair. He ran his hands through his curling hair and then tugged at his waistcoat. "Now, if you'll excuse me, I think I shall take a turn about the grounds myself. Perhaps I'll happen upon Jane and her aunt and uncle on their return from Lambton."

With a jaunty bow, Bingley exited the library, leaving Darcy alone with his thoughts.

Darcy let out a breath and crossed the room toward the overstuffed shelves. He browsed the leather bound volumes and finally selected a book on agricultural practices to pass the time until dinner. After the storms the tenant farmers would be readying themselves for the coming planting season—even if they would be late to begin it. There was still time to salvage the harvest if they moved quickly.

Which reminded him that he would have to return to the farms to lend his assistance—he had been far too distracted of late.

As he settled into his favorite armchair, his mind drifted back to his conversation with Elizabeth during their morning walk. Her inquiries about Amelia's parentage had been astute, and he admired her forthrightness in broaching the subject. It was clear that she took her role as the child's caretaker seriously and wished to understand the situation fully.

Yet, as much as he appreciated her candor, Darcy found himself troubled by the mystery surrounding Amelia's origins.

Who were her true parents?

And why had they chosen to leave her in his care?

The note had claimed she was a Darcy, but offered no further explanation.

It gnawed at him, this uncertainty, even as he resolved to provide for the child as best he could.

With a grunt, Darcy attempted to focus on the book in his hands, but found his thoughts repeatedly straying to a pair of fine eyes and a quick wit. It had only been one day since her arrival, and already Miss Elizabeth Bennet was proving to be quite the distraction, in more ways than one. Her intelligence and warmth had made an impression on him, and he found himself looking forward to their future interactions.

Yet, he chastised himself for allowing his mind to wander in such a direction. Elizabeth was here as Amelia's governess, and it would be entirely improper to view her as anything more. He must maintain a respectful distance and focus on his responsibilities as Amelia's guardian.

Nothing more.

elizabeth

ELIZABETH DID NOT MIND her change of scenery, in truth she had been seeking an escape from Longbourn and the pressure of her mother's constant scheming.

She had hoped that Jane's engagement to Mr. Bingley would quell some of Mrs. Bennet's fanatical interest in seeing her daughters married—if only for a short while—but it had, instead, made her all the more eager to see the rest of her daughters married and settled as quickly as possible.

Mr. Bingley's letter had arrived at precisely the right moment, and Elizabeth could not have been more grateful to the stranger who had offered her the position in a county far away from Hertfordshire at an estate that was far grander than anything she had ever laid eyes on.

As she had settled into the rhythm of the house, Elizabeth felt more at home in Pemberley where the only person who expected anything of her was Amelia... and she did not mind that at all.

It was not a hardship to take her meals with the servants, and she preferred it to the grandeur of the great dining room and the oppressive silence of the house.

The kitchens were familiar, warm, and comforting, and the company was delightful.

Mrs. Reynolds had, indeed, engaged a wet nurse for Amelia, and Elizabeth dearly loved talking with the young woman who had only recently arrived in Derbyshire from Scotland. Her story was an unfortunate one, but she seemed content to help care for Amelia and did not speak much about the life she had left behind her.

Mrs. Reynolds seemed to prefer that as well.

"Mrs. Reynolds," Elizabeth asked, "if I may—"

The housekeeper stopped and took a seat beside her at the table.

"Mr. Darcy— He is—"

Mrs. Reynolds' smile was indulgent. "The very best gentleman and master I could ask for," she said. "The kindest of men."

"I— That is wonderful to hear," Elizabeth said. "But I was not going to ask what sort of man he was—I feel that I have had a good impression of him..."

Mrs. Reynolds laughed. "That is a relief, Miss Bennet. Mr. Darcy is a stoic gentleman at the best of times, and he can be very... stern. But that is his way when he is not... When he does not know someone well enough to be himself."

"I see," Elizabeth replied with a smile. "I shall keep that in mind."

The housekeeper's eyebrow rose. "If that was not what you wished to ask—"

"I wished to ask about Amelia," Elizabeth said. "Her parentage—"

"Ah. It is a mystery, I am afraid," Mrs. Reynolds sighed. "She looks nothing like anyone in the portraits in the gallery... but I suppose she is too young to show any resemblance."

"And Mr. Darcy's sister—"

The housekeeper let out a snort. "No, indeed. Miss Georgiana is a proper young lady who would not think of shaming her family in such a manner."

Elizabeth's gaze flickered to the young Scottish woman nursing Amelia, but she did not look up. The housekeeper's judgement was pointed and Elizabeth felt immediately protective of the young woman.

"Indeed," she said. "I do not feel that we are in any position to judge such things. There was a young woman in Hertfordshire who was abandoned by a young man who was courting her—he disappeared one day. Some say he went away to join the militia, but not a month after he disappeared, the young lady was discovered to be with child."

Mrs. Reynolds let out a horrified gasp and out of the corner of her eye, she noticed the young woman glance in her direction.

"The young woman's father very proudly announced the child's birth, and the whole of Meryton was invited to his christening ceremony. She was married to a wonderful young man not long after and they are very happily married with a large family."

"How lovely," Mrs. Reynolds said, and Elizabeth hoped that she saw the older woman was somewhat chastized. But it did not matter, she wished only for the young Scottish woman to feel that she was not in the wrong and that she should not feel ashamed for her own circumstance.

"The young woman who brought Amelia to Pemberley might have been in the same situation," Elizabeth said. "Giving a child to someone who can give her a better life is an admirable thing... I only wish I knew who she was."

The housekeeper rose from her chair and smoothed her hands over her apron. "Well," she said. "Until we know such a thing, Miss Amelia is our charge and she shall be well cared for while she is under this roof." She looked around the room and her gaze fell upon the cook. "Is everything in readiness for tonight's dinner?" she asked.

The cook nodded and began to list off the foods that would be prepared and Elizabeth's stomach growled just a little despite the fact that she had just eaten.

Mr. Darcy had asked her to join him for dinner—perhaps Amelia would be asleep by then.

Once Amelia had been settled into her cradle with a maid set to watch over her, Elizabeth ventured out into the house to explore. She had missed visiting with the Gardiners while they had been in Lambton, and she had exclaimed over the fine lace that Jane had purchased at the market. Jane had mentioned in passing that their aunt and uncle would visit Pemberley, but Elizabeth was suddenly worried that she would miss their visit while she was preoccupied with Amelia. To that end, she sought out Mr. Darcy—the mention of the dinner party had reminded her that she did miss social interactions. Though she had been distracted by the child—and for good reason—Mr. Darcy would not wish for her to spend all of her time with Amelia. In fact, during their walk he had seemed truly disappointed that she would not be joining him for dinner that evening.

As she walked down the corridor, she heard voices coming from the parlor, and paused long enough to recognize Jane's light laughter as she spoke with Mr. Bingley.

However, she did not wish to disturb them and she moved quickly past the doorway in search of the master of Pemberley.

But as much as she searched, she could not find him.

Frustrated, she entered the library and walked to the window that looked out over the rolling fields of the estate.

All at once, she let out a gasp.

There, walking through the grass with his jacket slung over

his shoulder and his mud-spattered linen shirt untucked from his breeches, was Mr. Fitzwilliam Darcy. His boots were covered in mud and his dark hair was plastered to his forehead with sweat.

Where had he been?

When he disappeared around the side of the house, Elizabeth rushed to the foyer and flung open the door, but as she stepped out onto the landing, she could not see him.

Suddenly overcome with a need to know where precisely he had been, Elizabeth walked around the house with quick steps. As she came around the corner of the house, a movement in the garden caught her eye, and she looked toward it—and crashed into a solid object.

"Oh!"

She stumbled back a few steps, shaken and then looked up, angry with herself for not watching her steps—had she struck the side of the house?

No.

Mr. Darcy stood there, aghast.

"Miss Bennet—" he choked out.

He rushed forward to offer his arm to steady her, but Elizabeth batted his hand away. Her cheeks burned with embarrassment.

"I am quite well," she huffed. "I— I am sorry, I did not see you—"

The gentleman's eyes were bright from whatever exertion he had recently undertaken, and Elizabeth was struck by just how tall and imposing a figure he was.

"Where have you been?" she blurted out and then instantly regretted her words.

Mr. Darcy pushed a hand through his damp hair and grimaced. "I had hoped to enter the house without causing a stir," he said. "I have been to see the tenant farmers— they have had some trouble with the recent storms and I have been helping them to rebuild their houses and barns."

Did every gentleman do such labor for their tenants?

She could not ask such a question.

"Oh—"

"Was there something you needed," the gentleman asked. "Is Amelia well?"

"Yes," Elizabeth answered quickly. "Quite well. She is sleeping— one of the maids is watching her."

"Wonderful," Mr. Darcy replied.

They stood in silence for a moment, and Elizabeth cursed herself for her impulsive notion to rush out into the courtyard.

"I heard you were hosting a dinner party tonight?" she said.

His dark eyes lit up. "Indeed, I am. I hope that you will be able to join us—"

"Perhaps," she replied. "Who will be in attendance?"

"Mr. Bingley and your sister Jane, of course. As well as a few of my friends from Lambton. It shall be a most pleasant gathering. I have also extended an invitation to your aunt and uncle— I know they are staying in Lambton, but they are most welcome here at Pemberley before their journey takes them back to London."

"You are very gracious," Elizabeth said with some surprise. "So many people to attend to— Are you quite sure—"

Darcy raised a hand. "Think nothing of it. Pemberley has been very quiet for a very long time. Georgiana is always lecturing me for my solitude. Besides— it is only for a short while."

He paused and shifted his stance.

"Will you come to supper?"

Elizabeth smiled. "The party sounds delightful," she said. "I shall attend. But only for a little while, and I must leave if Amelia needs me."

"Of course," Darcy nodded. "Your dedication to her welfare is most admirable. Now— if you will excuse me, I must hide my muddy boots from Mrs. Reynolds' watchful eye."

Elizabeth suppressed a laugh as Darcy gave a small bow.

"I shall see you at supper," he said.

"Indeed," she replied.

* * *

ELIZABETH DID NOT ATTEND the supper, but when Amelia was finally settled into her cradle for the night, Elizabeth dressed carefully in the finest gown she had brought with her and ventured down to the main floor of the house.

Conversation and laughter echoed in the foyer and Elizabeth felt a swell of regret at having missed the earlier part of the evening. But it could not be helped.

Elizabeth took a steadying breath before entering the drawing room, where the dinner party had adjourned for after-dinner conversation and entertainment. As she stepped into the well-lit space, several pairs of eyes turned to regard her with curiosity and interest.

Mr. Darcy, who had been engaged in conversation with a gentleman Elizabeth did not recognize, immediately excused himself and crossed the room to greet her.

"Miss Bennet," he said warmly, a smile gracing his usually stoic features. "I am pleased you were able to join us, even if only for a short while."

Elizabeth returned his smile, feeling a flutter of nervousness in her stomach at being the center of attention. "Thank you, Mr. Darcy. I apologize for my late arrival."

"Think nothing of it," he assured her. "Come, let me introduce you to our guests."

Darcy guided Elizabeth around the room, making introductions to the assembled company. She was delighted to see her aunt and uncle, who greeted her with affectionate embraces and inquiries about her well-being and that of little Amelia. Jane and Mr. Bingley were also present, their faces aglow with the happiness of their recent engagement.

As the evening progressed, Elizabeth found herself drawn into lively conversations with Darcy's friends from Lambton, who proved to be engaging and welcoming. She was particularly taken with a Miss Emmeline Hartwell, a vivacious young woman with a keen wit and a love of literature that rivaled Elizabeth's own. The two quickly fell into an animated discussion of their favorite novels, much to the amusement of those around them.

They had only been sitting for a short time when Mrs. Rivers, an inquisitive neighbor with an insatiable appetite for gossip approached Mr. Darcy and Elizabeth glanced up as she swept through the room.

"Forgive my impertinence, Mr. Darcy, but I simply must know more about the baby left on your doorstep!" she declared, her eyes alight with curiosity. "The whole town is positively ablaze with questions about it!"

The room fell quiet, all eyes now on Darcy, who hesitated. Elizabeth's breath caught as he glanced in her direction and her conversation with Miss Hartwell was paused as everyone in the room waited for their host to reply.

Darcy's jaw tightened almost imperceptibly as he faced Mrs. Rivers, his expression carefully controlled. "I am afraid there is not much to tell, madam," he replied evenly. "The child was left in my care, and I have taken on the responsibility of providing for her welfare. Miss Bennet has been engaged as her governess."

Mrs. Rivers' eyes widened, her gaze darting between Darcy and Elizabeth. "But surely there must be more to the story!

Who are the child's parents? And why was she left at Pemberley?"

Elizabeth felt a surge of protectiveness for both Amelia and Mr. Darcy. She stood and moved to his side and met Mrs. Rivers' probing stare with a calm, steady gaze of her own.

"Mrs. Rivers," she began, her voice gentle but firm, "while I understand your curiosity, I am afraid the details of Amelia's arrival are a private matter. A *family* matter. What is important is that she is now under the care and protection of Mr. Darcy, who has shown great compassion and generosity in taking her in. You may be assured that she will want for nothing at Pemberley."

Darcy glanced at Elizabeth, surprise and gratitude mingling in his expression. He gave her a small nod of appreciation before addressing Mrs. Rivers once more.

"Miss Bennet is quite correct. The child's well-being is my primary concern. You may tell your friends that there is no scandal to be found here."

Mrs. Rivers' cheeks flushed at the gentle rebuke, but she forced a tight smile and nodded. "Of course, Mr. Darcy. Forgive my impertinence. I am sure you will provide excellently for the child."

With that, she turned and made her way to another group of guests, no doubt eager to share what little information she had gleaned.

Elizabeth let out a soft sigh of relief, grateful that the uncomfortable moment had passed.

"Thank you, Miss Bennet," he said quietly, his voice low enough for only her to hear. "Your intervention was most appreciated."

Elizabeth felt a warmth bloom in her chest at his words. "Think nothing of it, Mr. Darcy. It is my duty to protect Amelia, and by extension, your privacy. I will not allow idle gossip to tarnish your reputation or hers."

Darcy's lips twisted into a small smile. "You are a formidable ally, Miss Bennet. Amelia is fortunate to have you as her champion."

Their gazes held for a moment longer than was strictly proper, and Elizabeth felt a strange flutter in her stomach. She quickly looked away, her cheeks warming.

"I should return to my conversation with Miss Hartwell," she said, her voice slightly breathless.

"Of course," he said. "I shall not keep you from it—"

Elizabeth took a fresh glass of claret from a servant at the edge of the room and walked back to the couch where Miss Hartwell awaited her. While their conversation continued, Elizabeth found her gaze, and her thoughts, drifting back to Mr. Darcy. And she imagined that he might have been looking at her, too.

elizabeth

AFTER INTEREST in Amelia's history had died down and the evening had come to a close, Jane and Mr. and Mrs. Gardiner had gone up to their rooms. Clearly feeling the effects of the brandy he had drunk after dinner, Mr. Bingley bid them a cheerful goodnight a short while later, and Darcy and Elizabeth were left alone in the dimly lit parlor.

Darcy stood by the fire as Elizabeth remained seated on a velvet upholstered chair. Elizabeth was searching for something to say when the gentleman turned to her.

"Miss Bennet," he began in a serious tone, "I find myself unable to let the matter with Amelia rest—"

"What matter?"

"Mrs. Rivers is a notorious gossip," he replied. "But she will not be the only one asking questions. Will you aid me in discovering Amelia's parentage?"

She hesitated for a moment, her eyes searching for sincerity. Then she nodded. "Of course, Mr. Darcy. But how—"

Darcy's forehead creased. "I have only the letter that accompanied her..."

"But, surely—" Elizabeth paused. She did not wish to upset him or have her think she did not respect him. "Surely there are members of your family that could be considered? Your sister, I know, is not involved—"

Darcy said nothing and Elizabeth felt that she could press on.

"But what of your other relatives? A cousin perhaps?"

Darcy's expression grew pensive as he considered Elizabeth's question. "I suppose it is possible," he admitted slowly. "I have several cousins, though I am not particularly close with any of them. Miss Anne de Bourgh in Kent... but it could not be her. My aunt would never allow such a thing. But there is Colonel Fitzwilliam— he is the second son of my uncle, the Earl of Matlock, and he is the only one I see with any regularity."

Elizabeth nodded thoughtfully. "It might be worth making inquiries, discreetly of course, to see if any of them could shed light on the situation. Perhaps one of them knows something about Amelia's origins, even if they are not directly responsible."

"You may be right," Darcy agreed, but there was a hint of weariness in his voice. "Though I dread the thought of involving my family in this matter. My aunt, Lady Catherine de Bourgh, in particular, would be most displeased if she caught wind of any potential scandal."

"I understand your reluctance," she said softly. "But if we are to uncover the truth, we must explore every avenue. I will assist you in any way I can, and I promise to be the very soul of discretion."

A faint smile touched Darcy's lips at her words. "I have no doubt of that, Miss Bennet. Your handling of Mrs. Rivers tonight was proof enough of your tact and diplomacy. I am grateful to have you as an ally in this."

Elizabeth felt a flush of pleasure at his praise, but she quickly tamped it down. It would not do to let herself become too affected by Mr. Darcy's words, no matter how sincere they seemed. She had a duty to focus on Amelia and unraveling the mystery of her parentage, not on the admittedly handsome and intriguing master of Pemberley.

Clearing her throat slightly, Elizabeth stood and smoothed her skirts. "Well then, Mr. Darcy, perhaps we should begin by making a list of your relatives and considering which ones might be most likely to have knowledge of Amelia's origins. We can then determine the best way to approach them."

Darcy nodded, a glint of determination in his eye. "Agreed. I will start with Colonel Fitzwilliam. He is a man of honor and discretion. If he knows anything, I trust he will confide in me."

He paused, seeming to wrestle with his next words. "As for my aunt, Lady Catherine... I believe it would be best if I handle any inquiries in that quarter myself. She can be rather... formidable, and I would not wish to subject you to her scrutiny unnecessarily."

Elizabeth's curiosity was piqued by his hesitation, but she sensed it was a delicate subject. "As you think best, Mr. Darcy. I will follow your lead in this matter."

"Thank you, Miss Bennet." Darcy said. "I shall draw up a list — we will discuss it in the morning. Perhaps we might engage your sister and aunt in this matter as well."

Elizabeth nodded once more. "I do agree." She glanced at the clock on the mantel and smothered a gasp of surprise. "It is very late," she said. "I must relieve Clara of her duties. Goodnight, Mr. Darcy."

He bowed and met her gaze with an intensity that took her breath away. "Goodnight, Miss Bennet."

Elizabeth swept out of the room and rushed through the

corridor and up the stairs to the suite of rooms she had been given. The maid she had left to care for Amelia was sleeping in a chair by the fire. After checking on the baby, who also slept soundly, Elizabeth woke Clara gently and sent her back to her own quarters.

Alone at last, Elizabeth sank down into the chair and stared into the fire.

They would have to proceed with caution.

Whatever the solution to this mystery might be, there was sure to be scandal—and Elizabeth wished for none of that darkness to touch the child in her care.

She could only hope that the matter would be solved quickly...

Or, perhaps it would be better if the question of Amelia's parentage could be forgotten altogether.

But would Mr. Darcy be willing to raise another man's child as his own?

She did not believe that he would abandon the child. *Surely not.*

But to raise her as his own child— Would he remain unmarried and forgo his own chance at happiness to keep her?

Would he do such a thing?

"Problems for another day," she muttered as she rose from the chair to prepare for bed.

In the morning everything would look clearer.

THE FOLLOWING morning was clouded and the sunlight that filtered through the clouds was tinged with rain and shadows that flickered across the lace curtains that covered the drawing room windows.

The gentlemen stood by the fireplace with their coffee while Mr. Gardiner fussed with his pipe.

The ladies were crowded around Amelia's bassinet and Elizabeth watched her sister with an indulgent gaze. Jane was enamored of the tiny creature and spent many hours holding her and singing to her. Elizabeth was certain that it would not be long before Jane and Mr. Bingey started a family of their own.

"May I hold her?" Jane asked softly, her eyes twinkling with curiosity and tenderness as she gazed down at little Amelia resting peacefully in Elizabeth's arms. She held out her hands, and Elizabeth, with a gentle smile, passed the baby to her sister.

As Jane cuddled the baby close to her chest, Elizabeth looked to Mr. Darcy.

"Have you made the list?" she asked.

Mr. Darcy stepped away from the fire and met her gaze firmly.

"I have," he said.

"What is all this?" Mr. Gardiner asked as he tapped his pipe against the marble fireplace mantel.

"We are determined to discover Amelia's parentage," Elizabeth replied.

"If I am to claim her as my own child, I must know that I am free to do so," Darcy said firmly.

His words took Elizabeth by surprise, but she tried not to show it.

He had made his decision.

She did not need to wonder any longer.

"Of course, we shall do whatever we can to assist," Bingley said.

"Capital," Mr. Gardiner exclaimed. "Mrs. Gardiner and I have spent ample time in Lambton, and we have become quite familiar with the local gossip."

"More gossip," Jane said without looking up from Amelia's little face.

"I do not know if it is idle gossip." Mrs. Gardiner hesitated for a moment before continuing. "We had heard that there was a young woman who had been working at the inn in Lambton. She was said to have been with child, but then suddenly disappeared a few months ago. No one seems to know what became of her or the baby."

Elizabeth and Darcy exchanged a meaningful glance. *Could this be the clue they were searching for?*

"Did you hear anything more about this young woman?" Darcy asked, his brow furrowed. "A name perhaps, or any details about her circumstances?"

Mrs. Gardiner shook her head apologetically. "I'm afraid not, Mr. Darcy. The innkeeper was rather tight-lipped about the whole affair. He seemed quite keen to avoid any scandal or gossip associated with his establishment."

"It's a start, at least," Elizabeth said thoughtfully. "Perhaps we could make some discreet inquiries in Lambton, see if anyone else remembers this young woman or knows what became of her."

Darcy nodded in agreement. "Yes, I think that would be wise. We must tread carefully, though. I do not wish to stir up any more speculation or rumors than necessary."

"Of course," Mr. Gardiner said as he lit his pipe. "Discretion is key in these matters. We shall do our best to gather information without drawing undue attention."

"I must say, Darcy," Mr. Bingley interjected, "if the woman has truly disappeared, it is unlikely we will find further useful information here in Lambton. I propose that we travel to London and seek information there."

"True," Darcy mused, weighing the idea. "London could indeed provide us with a greater opportunity to uncover the truth. And I had hoped to call upon my cousin Colonel Fitzwilliam."

Elizabeth nodded. "I agree. London may yield more answers, and your cousin could prove a valuable source of information. When do you propose we depart?"

Darcy considered for a moment. "I believe we should make arrangements to leave within the week. That will give us time to make the necessary preparations and inquiries here before setting out."

"Excellent," Bingley said with enthusiasm. "I shall accompany you, of course. And perhaps Miss Bennet and Miss Elizabeth would care to join us as well? I'm sure Jane would appreciate the opportunity to visit the shops in London for her trousseau."

Jane looked up from Amelia, a delighted smile on her face. "Oh, that would be wonderful, Charles! I would very much enjoy the trip, and it would be a great comfort to have Lizzy with me."

Elizabeth glanced at Darcy. "If Mr. Darcy has no objection, I would be happy to accompany my sister. But my first priority must be Amelia's well-being. I cannot leave her behind."

Darcy met her gaze steadily. "I would not dream of separating you from your charge, Miss Elizabeth. Amelia will, of course, travel with us. I'm sure we can make suitable arrangements for her comfort and care during the journey."

"She will be very well looked after at Gracechurch Street," Mrs. Gardiner exclaimed. "I will not hear any argument against it. It has been far too long since I have had a baby in the house!"

"It seems we are settled," Darcy said.

"Wonderful," Charles exclaimed. "I shall write to Mr. Gray at once and see that rooms are prepared for you. You will not stay at the club, I will not hear of it."

Darcy chuckled at his friend's exclamation and Elizabeth

noticed Jane's smile as she observed Mr. Bingley's animated response.

London.

To truly plan for Amelia's future, they would have to discover her past—Elizabeth could only hope that such a thing would be possible.

darcy

UPON ARRIVING IN LONDON, the group separated. Charles Bingley returned to his townhouse while Jane and the Gardiners made for Gracechurch Street. Elizabeth reluctantly allowed Jane to take little Amelia with her as she wished to accompany Darcy to visit his cousin. Mr. Gardiner was happy to play escort, as he did not yet wish to return to the work that awaited him at his warehouses.

"Where exactly are we headed, Darcy?" inquired Mr. Gardiner as he adjusted his hat against the chilly London wind.

"Well, sir, my cousin Richard Fitzwilliam has a residence here in London, though I do not know if he will be in residence. He is often called away—" Darcy replied. "I believe he will be a good place to begin our search. He would hate for me to say such a thing, but he seems to have an ear for gossip— Our great aunt was a notorious collector of secrets, and she adored Fitzwilliam and always brought him along to her engagements as the other ladies of her acquaintance would tell him *everything*."

Elizabeth pressed her hand to her lips to stifle a laugh and Darcy found himself smiling, too.

It really was quite amusing.

He had often felt some pity for his cousin at being dragged to such events on the arm of their ancient aunt... but he suspected that if Fitzwilliam *didn't* enjoy it, he would have certainly found a reason not to attend.

As they crossed a bustling thoroughfare, Darcy caught sight of a fleeting figure in the crowd—a woman with dark, black hair and a hooded cloak who seemed to be shadowing their movements. He blinked and rubbed his eyes, convincing himself that it was merely a trick of the light. However, within the recesses of his mind, he could not shake the nagging doubt that perhaps they were being followed.

"Is everything quite alright, Mr. Darcy?" Elizabeth asked as she noticed his momentary distraction.

"Of course, Miss Bennet, just a slight disturbance in the crowd," Darcy said, masking his uncertainty with a reassuring smile. "Come, along, we are almost there."

His cousin was not the sort of man to take liberties with his position or his wealth—which he always maintained was not nearly enough—but the house in which he resided was imposing and it loomed above them like a predatory bird as they stood upon the sidewalk.

"Here?" Elizabeth breathed.

Darcy climbed the steps and knocked on the door, the sound echoing through the still air. After a few moments, Darcy raised his first again, but just as he was about to knock, the door was wrenched open revealing the disheveled figure of his cousin.

"Good lord," the Colonel cried. "William! What the devil are you doing here?"

Darcy glanced over his shoulder at Elizabeth, whose eyes were wide with shock and no small amount of amusement.

"You stink," Darcy said flatly.

His cousin laughed. "I do," he agreed. "Cards went on far too long last night—or this morning, I should say. But what are you doing here?"

"May we come in?" Darcy asked.

Richard laughed and stepped away from the door. "Of course! Please, please! Do not stand in the street, it is likely to rain at any moment!"

Darcy let out a sigh and gestured for his companions to enter the house ahead of him. Elizabeth's lips were pressed into a thin line, but he had a feeling that she liked the Colonel. He could certainly be entertaining when he wished to be.

"Who are these people?" Richard called out. "I did not know you had new friends in London!"

"May I introduce Miss Elizabeth Bennet and her uncle, Mr. Gardiner," Darcy said as they entered the parlor. "They have been assisting me in a matter of great importance..." his voice trailed off as he looked around the room. "What happened to the drawing room?"

His cousin seemed confused, but only for a moment.

"Ah, I had it moved. This is the parlor now. The drawing room is down the corridor— I had all the furniture thrown into the street. Terrible business. Now— What is this matter of great importance?"

Darcy declined the glass of brandy his cousin offered him, but Mr. Gardiner accepted it gratefully.

A thought crossed Darcy's mind at that moment—what if the child were Fitzwilliam's? He was known to have wild parties when he was not busy with his military commission. And he was often abroad and in the company of many women... But Darcy knew very well that his cousin was focused on securing a wealthy bride who could pull him from obscurity and into proper society. *He would not risk that with an ill-timed dalliance...*

"I know that you have a keen ear for gossip, cousin," he

began. "We are in search of information regarding any family members who may have recently had children."

The Colonel leaned against the fireplace and regarded him carefully. "*Our* family?"

"Yes," Darcy replied. "Our family."

Colonel Fitzwilliam sucked in a breath, blew it out, and took a thoughtful sip of brandy. "Cousin Marietta had a son not long ago—her third. Mama would not cease in talking about it, especially as they are so happily set up in the countryside just west of London. One of our third cousins—or perhaps it is a second cousin—recently had a child, but that may have been last Christmas..."

He rattled off a list of other relatives who were new parents, each of whom seemed content in their domestic lives. No one of interest. And no one of any close relation who might claim the Darcy name.

"Are there any who might be unsatisfied or discontented—" Elizabeth interjected, rightly sensing that Darcy was too polite to inquire further.

"Obviously!" Richard snorted. "There is always *someone* in this family who believes their dire circumstances to be more dire than everyone else's."

The Colonel drained the contents of his glass and set it down on the mantel with a *click*. He crossed the room to a dark wooden desk, pulled open a drawer, and rifled through its myriad contents. Moments later, he produced a letter. Its parchment was white and new compared to the others in the drawer, which were mostly yellowed with age or stained in some way.

"Here," Richard said brightly. "This one is an absolute tragedy. But you must read this aloud—"

Darcy unfolded the paper and began to read, though he wished that his cousin were not so dramatic. Especially in Miss Bennet's presence.

"Dear Sir," he read, "I find myself in need of urgent financial assistance, as I intend to enter into marriage. I require funds for the preparations and ceremony. I trust that you will find it in your heart to support me in this endeavor, after doing little to aid me at any other point in my lifetime. Your nephew, Jonathan Darcy." He paused and frowned down at the letter. "He has provided an address in Covent Garden."

"You may have already guessed that I never sent him a single farthing," Richard said. "My sister has said that since the day he was born, he was nothing but trouble. The entire family has disavowed him—and it is endlessly troubling that he has decided to use the Darcy name instead of his own. The fact I have not publicly rebuked him is something he should be grateful for. Though after his little missive, I suppose I should not be so magnanimous."

The air felt heavy as Darcy considered this new piece of the puzzle. He had not seen Jonathan since he was quite young. But it seemed that he had not taken any lessons from his upbringing. His father was a fine and upstanding gentleman with a good merchant trading business—and it seemed clear enough that Jonathan had not risen to the greatness that had been expected of him.

Darcy knew he was going to have to go in search of this young man to see if he knew anything about Amelia, even if that meant venturing into unsavory territory.

"This is what we had hoped for," Elizabeth said. "We must leave at once!"

"Under no circumstances will you accompany me to Covent Garden," Darcy declared. "You must return to Gracechurch Street at once. Bingley and I will venture to Covent Garden tomorrow."

Elizabeth's eyes flashed with indignation, and Colonel Fitzwilliam laughed.

"Oh, dear, William— You've upset the young lady."

Darcy shot his cousin a pointed look, and the Colonel covered his mouth to keep his laughter at bay.

"Very well," she murmured, though her disappointment was clear.

"I am keeping this letter," Darcy snapped as he tucked it into his waistcoat pocket.

"Of course," Richard replied with a dismissive wave of his hand. "I have no use for it. But do not ask me to accompany you. I have no interest in going down to the Garden."

Darcy couldn't blame him.

There was no telling what a man in Jonathan's position might do... and if he was desperate and confronted with news he did not wish to hear—

As they took their leave of the Colonel's grand house, Darcy felt that they were one step closer to unraveling the mystery that had brought them here. However, as the door shut behind them, a looming sense of dread descended upon him like a shadowy cloud, poised to obscure the path they intended to pursue.

* * *

THE SOFT HAZE of candlelight filled the parlor of Bingley's London townhouse, and Darcy did his best not to compare it to his favored sitting room at Pemberley. London had never agreed with him, but Charles seemed to thrive in the business of it—which made it all the more ridiculous that his friend had been so adamant about taking a house in the countryside.

The room was richly furnished with exquisite damask-patterned wallpaper, heavy dark velvet curtains, and an intricately carved mahogany mantelpiece that housed a crackling fire.

Darcy always found it a little stately for his tastes, but Charles had left the decorating to his sisters and claimed to have no say in the matter.

Jane Bennet had come from Gracechurch Street with Elizabeth, but they had left baby Amelia with Mrs. Gardiner. Darcy was somewhat disappointed not to be able to see the child, but there would be time enough for that later.

After supper, Jane, Bingley, and Elizabeth sat down at a polished card table to play at whist, and a lively game was underway. Charles was an overly dramatic card player, which seemed to delight the ladies to no end.

Darcy, his brow furrowed in concentration, sat apart from the rest, perusing Jonathan Barry's—but calling himself a Darcy—letter once more. He absently toyed with the golden signet ring on his finger as he did so. What had happened to drive the young man to such extremity? To beg for money—and for a marriage? But to whom? Had it all been a ruse? He did not wish to suspect that the young man was gambling or drinking... but Covent Garden was not a place one went to better oneself.

"Mr. Darcy," Elizabeth called out from the card table, "why is it that I cannot accompany you to Covent Garden tomorrow? Surely my presence would be of some assistance."

He looked up, not quite ready to discuss the matter, but all eyes at the table were turned toward him. Charles seemed ready to laugh and Darcy wondered if he had missed overhearing a pertinent part of their conversation.

He shifted in his seat and laid the letter on his knee. "Miss Bennet, Covent Garden is a place teeming with destinations of ill repute and characters most unsavory. It is no place for a young lady, especially one such as yourself," he explained. "I will not put you in harm's way."

"My uncle says that Covent Garden is not so terrible... but I do not believe he has been there in some time," she mused as she laid down a card. "Is it unusual for young Jonathan Darcy to frequent such places?"

"Hardly." Darcy sighed, rubbing the bridge of his nose. "My cousin tells me that Jonathan has always been somewhat...rebellious. He is one of the few members of the family whom we do not speak of with any measure of pride. The real surprise is his claim of marriage; I find myself questioning the accuracy of such a statement."

"A false marriage to claim some money," Jane exclaimed. "A scandal to be sure!"

"If he *is* Amelia's father, then let us hope that Jonathan's newfound sense of responsibility is genuine—" Elizabeth said.

A momentary lull settled upon the parlor, the crackling of the fire providing a soothing backdrop to the gentle murmurs of conversation. But Bingley's brow creased and he refused to turn back to the cards even though it was his turn to play.

"You know, Darcy, I do recall Jonathan—"

Darcy regarded him carefully. "Oh?"

"Yes, I remember once, when we were young men and I had just come into your acquaintance, he and I had a quarrel over something so trivial—a pocket watch, I believe—and he flew into such a rage! It took both of us quite some time to recover from that scuffle. Quite an aggressive lad."

"Ah, yes," Darcy nodded, recalling similar instances. "Jonathan has always been afflicted with a terrible temper. The Colonel complained quite often that he acted impulsively and cared little for the consequences. We would often say that it was a mercy he was the youngest of his nephews and there were others who were better than him who would inherit... I did often feel some pity for him."

"Is it safe for you to go in search of him?" Elizabeth asked. "What if he tries to do something to harm you?"

"Rest assured," Darcy replied, "Jonathan may possess a fiery disposition, but he has never had the courage to cross me. Should he ever dare to do—" He did not finish the sentence. Jonathan would be a fool to attack him, but he did not know what state of extremity the young man might be in. There was no way to predict what might happen.

"I hope you are right," Elizabeth said.

Elizabeth's expression grew pensive. "And if Jonathan is indeed Amelia's father, what then? Will he claim her as his own, or will he expect you to continue raising her?"

Darcy's jaw tightened. "If he is her father, and if he is truly committed to providing for her, then I must respect his right to do so. But I will not simply hand her over without assurances of his ability to care for her properly. And if he proves unwilling or unable..." He trailed off, his gaze distant.

"Then you will keep her at Pemberley?" Elizabeth asked her eyes searching his face.

Darcy met her gaze steadily. "Yes. I gave my word that I would protect and provide for Amelia, and I intend to honor that promise, no matter what we may discover about her parentage."

A small smile touched Elizabeth's lips, and Darcy felt a curious warmth bloom in his chest at what he saw as her approval of his statement.

"Well then," Bingley said, breaking the moment, "it seems we have our course of action. Darcy and I shall venture into Covent Garden tomorrow to seek out this elusive young man and see what light he may shed on the situation."

"And Jane and I shall remain at Gracechurch Street," Elizabeth said with a sigh, "waiting and worrying, I suppose."

Jane reached over and patted her sister's hand. "Lizzy, you know Mr. Darcy and Mr. Bingley are more than capable of handling this matter. We must trust in their judgment and abilities."

Elizabeth nodded, though her expression remained troubled. "I know you are right, Jane. It is just difficult to sit idly by when I feel I could be of some use."

"Your role in caring for Amelia is of the utmost importance," Darcy said earnestly. "She needs your love and attention now more than ever. That is where you can be of the greatest service."

Elizabeth met his gaze, and after a moment, her features softened. "You are right, Mr. Darcy. Amelia's well-being must be my primary concern. I shall endeavor to be patient and await your return with whatever news you may bring."

Darcy inclined his head gratefully. "Thank you for your understanding, Miss Bennet. I promise to keep you apprised of any developments in our search."

With that, the conversation turned to lighter topics, and the evening passed in pleasant companionship. Yet beneath the surface, an undercurrent of anticipation and uncertainty lingered, as all present knew that the events of the morrow could very well shape the course of little Amelia's future.

As the fire continued to crackle in the hearth, Darcy could not deny the growing affection he felt for Elizabeth Bennet—an emotion that both excited and terrified him. The future, once so certain, was now shrouded in mystery, but in that uncertainty lay the promise of love and family. And though he had never really considered it before, perhaps that would not be so bad after all.

darcy

DARCY HAD SPENT the day pacing the study as he wrestled with the hundreds of possible outcomes of this mission. If they were wrong, the search would begin again— but if they were right and his cousin had given them the name they needed— other problems would come from that.

And then there was what to say to the man.

Darcy had not seen Jonathan since he was a young man... What changes had the years wrought upon him? And what had driven him to use the Darcy name in such a way?

The sun was just beginning to set when Bingley and Darcy made their way through London toward Covent Garden. A carriage would have been ideal and could have carried them directly to the location they sought, but Darcy did not wish to make a spectacle, and they abandoned the carriage some distance away and walked the streets at a quick pace and their hands tight on their walking sticks.

"I do not like this," Charles muttered.

"Nor do I," Darcy replied.

He could not bring himself to think of Amelia being raised in such a place.

The air was thick with the scent of fresh produce as shopkeepers were closing their stalls for the day, heaving crates of fruits and vegetables onto their carts. The neighborhood was filled with a cacophony of shouts and the bustle of activity.

They continued through the market until they reached a narrow, dark alleyway. At its end stood a rundown boarding house, its once-whitewashed facade now marred by years of grime. The windows were cracked and boarded up in places, and the door hung crooked on its hinges.

"Are you certain this is the place?" Bingley asked, eyeing the building with apprehension.

"Unfortunately, I am quite certain. It is exactly the sort of place I would expect to find him," Darcy replied, taking a deep breath as they approached the door. They hesitated for a moment before pushing it open and stepping inside.

The interior of the boarding house was dark and musty. A woman, her face lined with age and hardship, looked up at them suspiciously from a battered armchair that had been pulled close to the small coal-lit fire.

"Can I help you gentlemen?" she asked, her tone guarded. Her eyes flicked over their fine clothes, clearly not accustomed to seeing such well-dressed individuals in her establishment.

Darcy straightened his shoulders. "We are looking for a man named Jonathan Darcy. He gave this address in a letter—"

"Oh, I have a Jonathan Darcy staying here alright," the woman said, nodding. "He's not here right now. But you'll likely find him at the pub up the road. That's where you'll always find him. I wouldn't go in there dressed like that if I were you, though. Someone's liable to rob you blind."

"Thank you for your warning," Darcy replied tightly. He reached into his pocket and pulled out a half crown, offering it to her. "May we leave our coats with you?"

Bingley spluttered something unintelligible but Darcy ignored him.

The woman eyed the coin, then nodded.

"Aye, but don't be long. I can't promise they'll still be here come morning if you're not back by then."

"Understood," Darcy said and placed the coin onto her upturned palm before he shrugged out of his coat and laid it on a nearby table. Bingley grumbled, but did the same.

As they stepped back out into the alleyway, their finery left with the old woman, Darcy's heart pounded strangely in his chest. The thought of uncovering the truth about Amelia's parentage both excited and terrified him. Perhaps it would have been better not to know...

"Let us find this pub and get the answers we seek," Darcy said. "We will not leave until we have them."

A faint odor of dampness and decay wafted through the air as they approached the establishment—there were several taverns on the street, all of them filled with patrons. They would check them all if necessary, but this one was the closest —within stumbling distance of the boarding house.

The dreary exterior gave them pause, but as they had made it this far, it seemed pointless to turn back now.

Bingley's usual easy going demeanor had been replaced by a look of apprehension and Darcy hoped that his friend did not regret his decision to accompany him on this mission.

Upon entering the dimly lit pub the stench of stale ale and unwashed patrons assaulted his senses. He spotted a young man who bore a striking resemblance to his cousin Richard hunched over at a corner table, an empty glass clutched in his trembling hand. Jonathan. It had to be. His slovenly and drunken state was a disgrace to the Darcy name. His once fine clothes hung off his frame, stained and wrinkled beyond repair. His hair was matted and unkempt, giving him an air of dishevelment that repulsed Darcy. Most alarming though, were Jonathan's bloodshot eyes, swimming in pools of unshed tears, hinting at a despair that went beyond mere intoxication.

"Look at him," Darcy muttered to Bingley. "How far he has fallen, Bingley. I do not think he should know about Amelia. Not yet, that is. We do not know for sure that he is Amelia's father. And if he is, he is in no fit state to care for her."

"Indeed, he has fallen quite far," Bingley replied. "But remember, we are here to inquire about the letter and his marriage, not to reveal Amelia's existence. There will be time enough for that later."

"Agreed."

Darcy took a quick breath to steady himself before he strode towards their inebriated quarry.

"Jonathan Barry," Darcy began.

The young man looked up at them in bleary surprise.

"We have come seeking answers to certain... matters that have arisen," Darcy continued.

"Who're you?" Jonathan slurred, squinting at the two gentlemen before him. "And what d'you want from me?"

"Your letter to Richard Fitzwilliam. Your uncle," Bingley cut in, his patience clearly already tested. "The one requesting funds for your marriage."

"Marriage?" Jonathan hiccuped. His brow furrowed in confusion. "What marriage? Why'd y'care 'bout that?"

"Enough, Jonathan," Darcy interjected, increasingly aware of the heads that turned in their direction and the curious stares of the other patrons. "This is a matter of great importance, and we cannot afford your drunken senselessness. Sober up and tell us the truth!"

As Darcy's words seemed to penetrate Jonathan's foggy mind, a semblance of clarity returned to his bleary eyes. He blinked several times, as if to focus what remained of his senses.

"Fine," he muttered. He set down his empty glass with a thud and stared into the dregs of his drink. "Who knew a woman could cause such trouble? I haven't seen her in a year—and good riddance, I say."

"Who are you speaking of?" Darcy pressed, his patience wearing thin. "What woman? Were you engaged to be married?"

"Caroline," Jonathan finally choked out. "Miss Caroline Eugenia Bingley... A dark angel..." He took a breath and a crooked smile creased his once handsome face. "She was the most wonderful—and the most attentive—and then she left me without so much as a word!"

"Caroline?" Charles gasped, his face paling at the revelation. "How could my *sister* be involved with such a reprobate? Liar! I cannot believe it!"

Darcy laid a hand on his friend's arm. "Calm yourself, Charles— We must not make a scene," he hissed.

"Believe what you want," Jonathan retorted, his voice barely audible. "But it is the truth." Jonathan sighed and slumped in his chair. "It doesn't matter— She has gone now, anyway."

"Are you certain this is the truth, Jonathan?" Darcy demanded angrily. "Surely you must have confused her with someone else. Tell us something to prove it."

"Caroline Bingley, I give you this bracelet as a promise," Jonathan mumbled before he fell forward and collapsed onto the table, his head buried in his arms. Darcy stared at him incredulously for a moment, and then a loud snore emerged from the slumped figure.

"What—"

Charles Bingley's face was red with anger and confusion and Darcy was certain he had never seen his friend quite so discomposed.

Caroline Bingley had endeavored for years to ensnare Darcy

himself into marriage, but she had failed. The thought of Caroline Bingley being tied to his family in this way was inconceivable—and yet, here was Jonathan swearing it was true.

"Come, Bingley," Darcy said quietly. "There is nothing more we can do here."

Charles stormed out of the tavern before Darcy could stop him, and Darcy gritted his teeth as he sprinted after his friend. The door slammed loudly behind them as they burst out into the dark London night.

"Wait, Charles!" Darcy called out as he grabbed his friend's arm. "We cannot jump to conclusions—we do not know anything for certain yet."

"Unhand me, Darcy," Charles muttered through gritted teeth as he jerked his arm free from Darcy's grasp. "I cannot think for the blood that is pounding in my ears."

With that, Bingley turned on his heel and stalked off into the shadows, leaving Darcy standing there, feeling helpless and conflicted.

Darcy returned to the boarding house to collect their coats and left his address with the woman in the armchair with a request that she send word when Jonathan returned to his rooms.

With that, Darcy began the long walk back to the waiting carriage, contemplating the unsettling revelation they had just uncovered.

Could it be true?

Was it possible that Amelia was the daughter of Caroline Bingley and Jonathan Barry?

Had he used the Darcy name to convince her of his connection to the family?

The thought sent an icy shiver down his spine, but there had to be more to the story; he was determined to discover it.

* * *

"BUT CHARLES, are you certain of this?" Jane asked.

Elizabeth and Jane sat side by side on the couch in Bingley's parlor.

Little Amelia was nestled in a bassinet by the fireside, sleeping peacefully, and they did their best to keep their voices low so as not to wake her.

"Caroline is Amelia's mother," Bingley spoke through gritted teeth as he paced back and forth like a caged lion. "How could she *do* such a thing? To have a child with that scoundrel— and then abandon her!" He clenched his fists, his knuckles turning white.

"When was the last time you saw your sister, Charles?" Elizabeth asked gently.

"Over a year ago," Bingley replied, his anger momentarily abating. "I learned that she had been entangled with some rather unsavory characters—" He paused for just a moment and Darcy could see the pain etched in his friend's features. He had mentioned none of this to him.

"There were some gambling debts that never seemed to be repaid even though I sent her enough money to do so... and then she stopped replying to my letters. I tried reaching out to her, but it was as if she had vanished into thin air." His voice trembled slightly, betraying his fear for his elder sister's well-being.

Darcy caught Elizabeth's gaze, his own eyes narrowing in suspicion.

"I cannot help but wonder if Jonathan played a part in Caroline's downfall," he mused aloud. "The fact that he was using the Darcy name— Perhaps he misled and lied to her to gain her trust and affection."

"Surely it is not in Caroline's nature to behave in such a manner," Jane said.

A wry expression twisted Bingley's features. "Unfortunately," he said. "My sister is somewhat of a scoundrel herself. She gambles too much, and drinks almost as much as Louisa's husband—"

Jane and Elizabeth exchanged pointed looks before focusing on Charles once more.

Charles let out a strange, hollow laugh. "Do you know, I was actually glad that I had not spoken to her in so long," he said. "I feared that she might reappear to ruin everything that I had achieved at Netherfield Park—that she might... do whatever she could to sully my dream... and that she might have tried to come between me and my dear Jane..."

"But she was waylaid by Jonathan—steered off course," Darcy said. Inwardly, he cursed himself for not keeping a closer watch on his family's activities and wondered if he might have been able to intervene to prevent this tragic turn of events.

Elizabeth's brow furrowed in thought, her gaze drifting towards the sleeping infant nestled in a bassinet near the fire.

"Caroline must have been truly desperate to leave her child like this. Perhaps we should trust that she did what she thought was best for Amelia, given the circumstances."

"Best for the child?" Bingley scoffed, his anger flaring once more. "Abandoning her is hardly what I would call 'best'! She could not come to me, her brother? I— I will not—" He turned on his heel and stormed out of the room and his footsteps echoed in the corridor.

Jane glanced at Darcy, her gentle eyes filled with concern.

"I should go check on Charles," she murmured, rising from the settee with a swish of silk skirts. Elizabeth squeezed her sister's hand reassuringly before releasing it and watched as Jane slipped out of the room after her distraught fiance.

The sudden quietness of the parlor was only punctuated by the soft crackle of the fire. Darcy moved closer to Elizabeth, their mutual concern for the child drawing them together. She leaned against the arm of the couch, a soft smile upon her face as she looked down at the child. As the silence enveloped them, Darcy felt the stirrings of an idea forming in his mind—one that might help them unravel the mystery of Caroline's disappearance and secure young Amelia's future.

Elizabeth glanced up at him, her eyes searching for answers he did not yet possess. "Mr. Darcy," she began, "what can we do to help Charles, and by extension, poor little Amelia?"

His mind seized upon the idea he had been considering, and he turned to face her fully.

"Caroline kept a house in London," he said. "It is further uptown, and Bingley's grandfather lived there until his death— Caroline would go there quite often to care for him and keep him company, and the property is still owned by Bingley's family. Perhaps we could go there tomorrow and see if she has left anything behind that would give us a clue to her whereabouts."

Elizabeth's eyes brightened with hope.

"An excellent plan," she agreed. "I will ask my Uncle Gardiner to accompany us. Jane can stay here and console Charles, and my aunt will be very eager to look after Amelia. She has grown very fond of her."

"Very well," Darcy nodded, appreciating her decisive nature. "We shall endeavor to solve this mystery tomorrow."

As he stood there, something stirred deep within Darcy's chest, a tenderness he had not allowed himself to feel before. He hoped, perhaps against reason, that their united efforts would bring about positive change for all involved—especially young Amelia.

elizabeth

ACQUIRING her uncle's agreement to accompany them uptown had not taken much convincing. Mr. Gardiner had developed a fierce fondness for Amelia and seemed to be just as invested in her future as Elizabeth.

Mr. Darcy had seemed more silent and thoughtful than usual during their carriage ride, and Elizabeth dearly wished to know what thoughts tumbled through his mind.

Since learning that Charles Bingley's troubled sister could be Amelia's mother, Elizabeth's own thoughts had been troubled. Why had she brought the child to Pemberley instead of to her own brother?

As the carriage rumbled along the cobblestone streets, Elizabeth found herself stealing glances at Mr. Darcy's pensive face. His brow was furrowed, and his eyes held a distant look as if he were deeply lost in thought. She longed to reach out, to offer some comfort or reassurance, but propriety held her back.

Uncle Gardiner cleared his throat, breaking the heavy silence. "So, Mr. Darcy, what exactly do you hope to find at Miss Bingley's residence?"

Darcy seemed to shake himself from his trance. "In truth, I

am not entirely certain. But I hope that we might uncover some clue as to her whereabouts—or her state of mind when she left Amelia at Pemberley. Perhaps a letter or a journal that could shed light on her motivations."

Elizabeth nodded. "It is a slim hope, but one worth pursuing. I cannot fathom why she would not turn to her own family in her time of need, especially with a child to consider."

"Pride, perhaps," Darcy mused. "Or fear of judgement and censure. The Bingleys are a respectable family, and an illegitimate child would certainly cause a scandal."

"But to abandon her own flesh and blood?" Elizabeth shook her head. "It seems so cold, so heartless."

"Desperation can drive people to do things they never thought themselves capable of," Uncle Gardiner said sagely.

"Caroline has always been an impulsive and unpredictable sort of woman," Darcy said. "There is nothing I do not believe her to be capable of... even something heartless."

Elizabeth sensed there was more that he wished to say, but could not bring himself to do so.

"I believe that Jonathan may have led Caroline to believe that he was more closely related to me than he really is," Darcy continued. "If she had known the truth about his family, there is no telling what she might have done—"

The carriage came to a halt in front of a modest but well-kept townhouse. As they alighted, Elizabeth noticed the curtains twitch in an upstairs window, as if someone had been watching their arrival.

"It appears the house is not entirely unoccupied," she murmured to Darcy as they alighted from the carriage.

Darcy's jaw tightened. "Let us hope it is merely a servant and not Caroline herself. I am not certain I am prepared for a confrontation just yet."

Uncle Gardiner knocked firmly on the door, and after a

moment's pause, it swung open to reveal a stern-faced house-keeper. Her eyes widened slightly as she took in the well-dressed visitors on the doorstep.

"May I help you?" she asked, her tone guarded.

"Good day, madam," Darcy said, stepping forward. "I am Mr. Fitzwilliam Darcy, a friend of the Bingley family. We have come to inquire after Miss Caroline Bingley."

The housekeeper's expression remained impassive. "I'm afraid Miss Bingley is not in residence at present. She has been away for some time."

"I see," Darcy replied, exchanging a glance with Elizabeth. "And do you know when she is expected to return?"

"I cannot say, sir," the housekeeper replied.

"May we come in?" Darcy asked.

The housekeeper's eyes narrowed.

"We will only be a moment," Elizabeth said. "Please, there is a great deal at stake— A matter of urgency."

The housekeeper hesitated, her gaze darting between Elizabeth's pleading expression and Darcy's determined one. After a long moment, she stepped aside, allowing them to enter.

"Very well," she said reluctantly. "But I must insist that you do not linger. My mistress would not approve of uninvited guests."

"We shall be brief," Darcy assured her as they stepped into the foyer.

The interior of the house was tastefully decorated, but there was a distinct air of neglect, as if it had been some time since anyone had truly lived there. A fine layer of dust coated the surfaces, and the air held a slight musty odor.

"Miss Bingley's chambers are upstairs," the housekeeper said, gesturing towards the staircase. "I trust you will respect her privacy."

"Of course," Elizabeth replied, offering the woman a reassuring smile.

The housekeeper nodded curtly and withdrew, leaving them to ascend the stairs on their own.

As they entered Caroline's bedchamber, Elizabeth was struck by the opulent furnishings as well as the sense of abandonment that permeated the space. The bed was made, but various articles of clothing lay strewn about, as if Caroline had left in a great hurry.

Darcy moved toward the writing desk, his eyes scanning the scattered papers for any hint or clue that might lead them to Caroline's whereabouts. Elizabeth and her uncle began carefully searching through the armoire and dressing table, mindful not to disturb the contents too greatly.

As Elizabeth sifted through a drawer filled with ribbons and lace, her fingers brushed against something hard and cold. Puzzled, she gently extracted the object—a delicate silver bracelet, its links tarnished with age and neglect. A small moonstone was inset in the center link and as Elizabeth turned the bracelet over in her hand, she noticed that it was engraved with the initials *C.E.B.*

"Mr. Darcy," she called softly, holding out the bracelet. "Look at this. Could this be the bracelet you mentioned— The one Jonathan spoke of?"

Darcy turned from the desk, his brow furrowed as he examined the piece of jewelry. "It very well could be. The initials certainly match Caroline's name. And if Jonathan's drunken ramblings hold any truth, this may have been a token of affection between them."

Uncle Gardiner peered over Elizabeth's shoulder and studied the bracelet with interest. "A promise, perhaps? Given in lieu of a ring to signify an understanding between a couple."

Elizabeth nodded, her mind racing with possibilities. "If

Caroline truly believed Jonathan's claims about his connection to the Darcy family, she may have seen this as a promise of marriage and security—perhaps even his wealth. But when the truth came to light, she must have felt betrayed and desperate."

"Desperate enough to abandon her own child," Darcy said grimly, his expression darkening. "Though I still cannot fathom such an action, no matter the circumstances."

"Nor can I," Elizabeth agreed, her heart aching for little Amelia. "But this bracelet does seem to lend credence to Jonathan's story, as unsavory as it may be."

Uncle Gardiner cleared his throat. "I hate to be the one to suggest it, but do you think there is a possibility that Caroline may have...taken her own life? The shame and despair of her situation, coupled with Jonathan's deception..."

A heavy silence fell over the room as they contemplated the grim possibility. Elizabeth felt a chill run down her spine at the thought.

Darcy shook his head. "No, I do not believe Caroline would resort to such an action. She is too proud, too resilient. If anything, I believe she has gone into hiding to avoid the scandal and to start anew somewhere else. Perhaps on the Continent... or the Colonies where no one would know her past."

"I pray you are right, Mr. Darcy," Elizabeth said softly. "For Amelia's sake, and for Mr. Bingley's. To lose a sister in such a way would be a devastating blow."

Just then, Elizabeth noticed something protruding from beneath the mattress on the carefully made bed. She laid the bracelet in Darcy's hand and walked over to it.

Elizabeth knelt beside the bed and pulled a small leather-bound journal from between the mattress and the frame, its pages slightly crumpled as if it had been hastily hidden away.

"It appears to be Caroline's diary," Elizabeth said as she opened it gently and turned to the last page. "The last entry is dated just over a year ago, right around the time Amelia would have been born."

"What does it say?" Darcy asked, and it sounded as though he was almost afraid to hear the answer.

"April 23rd," Elizabeth began softly. "I cannot fathom how my life has come to this point. When I agreed to marry Jonathan, I believed him to be a gentleman of character, but I was grievously mistaken. He is nothing more than an abusive brute, and I regret ever agreeing to be his wife."

Beside Mr. Darcy, whose expression was twisted in anger, Mr. Gardiner shifted uncomfortably, his mouth tight with concern.

"Is there more?" Darcy asked quietly.

Elizabeth hesitated, her eyes scanning the pages before her. "There is much more, but most of it details the horrors she experienced at the hands of the man she intended to marry. It is... difficult to read."

"Perhaps we should focus on anything that might pertain to her disappearance or the child," Mr. Gardiner suggested gently.

"Yes," agreed Darcy but his gaze never left Elizabeth's face. "We must discover the truth, however painful it may be."

"Very well," Elizabeth said. She took a deep breath before flipping through the pages, her brow furrowed in concentration. "Ah, here is something that may be of interest."

"Please, proceed," Darcy urged.

"June 14th," Elizabeth read, her voice faltering slightly. "I have made the decision to leave Jonathan. I cannot bear the thought of our child growing up in such a dangerous environment. My heart aches at the thought of leaving my family, but I know that it is for the best."

"How horrible it must have been for her," Mr. Gardiner said under his breath.

"Listen to this," Elizabeth said. "Caroline writes, 'I hid away and had the baby in secret so Jonathan would never know, as I did not trust him around an infant.' Oh, Mr. Darcy. How awful."

"Horrible," Mr. Gardiner muttered.

"Here is another entry," Elizabeth continued, her voice trembling slightly. "'I have been given the opportunity to escape Jonathan's violence and flee to America. But the trip across the ocean seems perilous, and I fear for Amelia's safety. I have decided to leave my precious child at Pemberley—Charles would never forgive me if he knew, but Mr. Darcy is of a different character. He should have been Amelia's father—'"

Elizabeth glanced up at Mr. Darcy, but the gentleman had turned away.

"Perhaps now Charles will understand why his sister did what she did," Elizabeth said softly as she closed the book and rose to her feet.

"We can only hope," Mr. Gardiner said.

"It is our duty to ensure Amelia's safety and happiness," Darcy said. His tone was strange, but Elizabeth could sense his anguish. Had he and Caroline Bingley been intended for one another at some point? Did he feel some guilt or responsibility for what had happened?

It was not his fault—that much was certain.

"Mr. Darcy," Elizabeth began, "we must do everything in our power to protect Amelia from her father. If he were to ever discover—"

"You have my word," Darcy vowed.

"But what is to be done about Caroline?" Elizabeth asked. "If she is in the colonies—"

Darcy's hand closed over the tarnished silver bracelet. "If she has truly fled to America, it will be difficult to track her down. The colonies are vast, and she could be anywhere."

Elizabeth nodded. "And even if we were to find her, would it be wise to bring her back? The scandal and shame she would face here in London could be too much to bear."

"Perhaps it is best to let her start anew," Mr. Gardiner mused. "A chance at a fresh beginning, away from the pain and suffering she must have endured at Jonathan's hands."

Darcy's expression was stern. "I agree that we should not actively seek to bring Caroline back against her will. But I do believe we have an obligation to inform Charles of his sister's fate."

"Of course," Elizabeth said. "Mr. Bingley deserves to know the truth, however painful it may be. I only hope that Caroline will come to understand that her family will always welcome her if she chooses to come home."

"We must also take steps to ensure that Jonathan never discovers Amelia's whereabouts," Darcy said firmly. "I will not allow that scoundrel anywhere near the child— Nor will I permit him to sully the Darcy name any further."

Mr. Gardiner placed a comforting hand on Darcy's shoulder. "We will do all we can to protect Amelia and keep her safe," Mr. Gardiner assured Darcy.

Darcy's smile was brief but genuine. "Thank you, Mr. Gardiner. I cannot tell you how grateful I am for your assistance."

Elizabeth clutched Caroline's diary to her chest, her heart heavy with the knowledge of the suffering the young woman had endured. She had never met Caroline, but that did not mean she could not empathize with her.

"Poor Caroline," she murmured. "I cannot imagine the desperation and fear she must have felt. To be driven to such lengths..."

"It is a tragic situation," Darcy agreed solemnly. "But we must focus on the present and do what is best for Amelia. She is our priority now."

Mr. Gardiner cleared his throat. "Perhaps we should take the diary and any other personal effects. I am certain that Mr. Bingley would appreciate it."

Darcy and Elizabeth agreed readily. They quickly gathered a few more items—a locket with a miniature portrait, a stack of letters tied with a ribbon, and a small painting of a countryside scene that Darcy remarked upon as having seen it in Bingley's house when they were younger men.

As they made their way downstairs, the housekeeper emerged from a side room, her expression wary.

"Did you find what you were looking for?" she asked, eyeing the items in their hands.

"Yes, thank you," Darcy replied politely. "We appreciate your allowing us entry. If Miss Caroline returns, will you please send word to Mr. Bingley in Mayfair?"

The housekeeper nodded and a flicker of understanding passed over her features. "Of course, sir. I will keep you informed."

With that, they took their leave of the townhouse and stepped out into the bustling London street.

The carriage awaited them, and as they climbed inside, a somber mood settled over the group.

Elizabeth's mind raced with the revelations they had uncovered. Caroline's tragic tale, her desperate flight, and the heart-wrenching decision to leave her child at Pemberley weighed heavily on her conscience.

Darcy, too, seemed lost in thought, his brow furrowed and his lips pressed into a thin line. Elizabeth could only imagine the conflicting emotions he must be grappling with—the shock of discovering Amelia's true parentage, the anger towards Jonathan for his deceit and cruelty, and his promise to protect Amelia at all costs.

darcy

CHARLES PACED the length of the Gardiner's parlor, his eyes downcast as he absorbed the weight of everything Darcy and Elizabeth had told him. Charles clenched his fists and Darcy could sense the fury that boiled beneath his friend's calm exterior.

"Caroline... she must have been so frightened," he muttered, his voice laced with guilt and anger. "I should have seen the signs. I should have protected her."

Darcy watched his friend's torment with sympathy. He knew all too well the feeling of helplessness that came when one failed to protect a loved one.

"None of us suspected Jonathan capable of such nefarious deeds, or that Caroline had fallen so far. But now that we know the truth, we must act."

"I cannot disagree— But what... What do you propose we do about it?"

"First, we shall find Jonathan and make him answer for his heinous actions." Darcy said firmly.

Elizabeth, who sat quietly in an armchair nearby, looked up

with concern. "But what if you put yourselves in danger by confronting him? For Amelia's sake—you must not be reckless."

"Rest assured, we shall take every precaution," Darcy replied, offering her a reassuring smile. The thought of putting her or Amelia in harm's way was unbearable to him.

"Reckless or not," Charles interjected, his anger now directed exclusively at Jonathan, "I wish to shake my fist in that scoundrel's face and demand justice for my sister!"

"Charles, I understand your anger," Darcy said in the hope of calming his friend. "But we must be cautious in our approach. It would be wise to wait until morning before taking any action."

At that moment, the faint sound of baby Amelia's fussing reached their ears. Elizabeth rose from her chair, concern etched on her face, but Darcy stopped her with a gentle hand on her arm.

"Allow me," he said softly, his eyes locked onto hers. "I will tend to her."

With a grateful nod, Elizabeth sat back down. "Her cradle has been placed in the drawing room," she said and Darcy inclined his head as he left the room.

He had already made up his mind as to how he would approach Jonathan—and if Charles were not so angry it might even be preferable to forget the truth they had discovered.

Darcy quietly entered the dimly lit drawing room which had been transformed into a makeshift nursery for their visit. His heart swelled with affection as he approached Amelia's crib. The baby's cries had softened to gentle whimpers, her tiny hands grasping at the air as if searching for comfort. Darcy reached down, tenderly lifted the infant into his arms, and cradled her close to his chest.

"Hush now, my dear," he whispered softly. He began to hum a soothing melody that had once brought solace to his own childhood fears. To his amazement, Amelia's eyes met his, a flicker of recognition in their depths, as she began to calm under his care.

The door creaked open and Elizabeth stepped hesitantly into the room.

"I am amazed at how much she takes to you," she murmured.

Darcy smiled faintly and continued to rock the child gently as he replied, "Perhaps she senses that she is safe and loved in our company. She behaves the same way with you, does she not?"

As his last words faded away, Amelia's eyelids fluttered closed, her breaths now deep and even. Carefully, Darcy laid her back in the cradle and tucked the soft blanket around her snugly.

"Miss Bennet, I must tell you how much your presence here means to me," he said as he straightened. "Over these past weeks, you have brought light into the darkest corners of my life. I— I cannot thank you enough for your assistance, both with Amelia and with this... terrible business."

Elizabeth's eyes softened as she gazed back at him. "It is *I* who should be thanking you. You have shown such kindness and generosity— Not only to Amelia but to my family as well. I am honored to play a role in ensuring her well-being and uncovering the truth of her origins."

She stepped closer, drawn by the tender expression on his face as he looked down at the sleeping child. "And I must confess, I have grown rather fond of Amelia myself. She has captured my heart in a way I never expected."

Darcy's breath caught at her nearness, but he could not bring himself to speak.

Elizabeth's eyes were on the sleeping child.

"I must ask you," she began. "What— What do you plan to

do? Will you give Jonathan the option of raising his child? And what of Mr. Bingley? Should he not, as the child's uncle, take on her care?"

Darcy considered Elizabeth's questions carefully before responding. "In truth, I do not believe Jonathan has any right to raise Amelia, given his abusive treatment of Caroline and his overall character. It would be irresponsible and dangerous to place her in his care."

He glanced down at the sleeping infant. "As for Charles, while he is indeed her uncle, I fear the revelation of his sister's secret and the scandal it could bring may be too much for him to bear at present. He is already grappling with the shock and guilt of not having been there to protect Caroline. And his marriage to your sister—I would not have their union sullied by gossip or societal pressures. I cannot even begin to guess how Charles' eldest sister, Louisa, would react."

Elizabeth frowned. "I know Jane would not argue if he did decide to take her into his home... However, I do understand if he could not do so... What, then, will you propose?"

Darcy took a deep breath. He had been considering this most carefully, but their discovery at Caroline's former home had forced him to consider it more seriously. "I have grown exceedingly fond of Amelia myself," he said, "and I cannot bear the thought of her being raised by anyone other than those who truly love and cherish her. If Charles is not ready or able to take on the responsibility, then I am prepared to raise her as my own daughter."

Elizabeth's eyes widened in surprise, but a smile played at the corners of her mouth. "You would do that? Take on the role of her father, despite the potential for gossip and speculation?"

"I would," Darcy said firmly, his gaze unwavering. "Amelia's well-being and happiness are paramount. Pemberley is removed enough from society that her presence would not raise any questions that could not be answered quite easily. And I care not for such things."

Elizabeth was silent, and Darcy worried that he had said something to upset her, but then a smile touched the corners of her mouth and his worry melted away.

"You are a man of great integrity, Mr. Darcy," Elizabeth said softly. "Amelia could not ask for a better guardian or a more loving home than the one you offer."

Darcy felt a rush of warmth at her words, a sense of rightness settling over him. "I only hope that I can provide her with the stability and affection she deserves. And I would be most grateful if you would consider continuing in your role as her governess and caretaker. Your presence has been invaluable... not only to Amelia but to me as well."

Elizabeth's breath caught, but she did not falter. "I would be honored, Mr. Darcy," she answered at once. "Amelia has captured my heart, and I cannot imagine being parted from her now."

Darcy's heart swelled with gratitude and affection at Elizabeth's ready agreement. The thought of raising Amelia together, and of building a life and family at Pemberley, filled him with a sense of hope and purpose he had not known before.

"Thank you, Miss Elizabeth," he said, his voice thick with emotion. "Your presence will be a blessing to us both."

Their gazes held, a silent understanding passing between them. At that moment, the future seemed bright and full of promise. Despite the confrontation that lay ahead of him, Darcy knew that *this* would be his reward.

The tranquil moment was broken by the sound of footsteps approaching. Darcy and Elizabeth turned as Charles paused in the doorway. "May I speak with you?" he hissed.

Darcy glanced at Elizabeth and crossed the room with quick

strides. He did not wish to wake the child and pulled the door closed behind him as he stepped into the corridor.

"Darcy, I have been thinking," Charles began without preamble. "I believe it is my duty to confront Jonathan and demand answers for his treatment of my sister— Even though I have not spoken to her, and she is beyond his reach and mine, I cannot in good conscience allow him to escape the consequences of his actions."

Darcy nodded, understanding his friend's need for justice. "I agree, Charles. But we must approach this with caution and a clear plan. We cannot risk putting ourselves in harm's way."

"Of course," Charles agreed. "But I will not rest until that scoundrel is held accountable for the pain he has caused my sister—"

"Tomorrow morning," Darcy said. "It is too late now, and I do not wish to enter that place after nightfall."

Charles nodded, but his jaw was tight. "As you say."

Darcy laid his hand on Charles' shoulder. "Have patience, we shall face him once more and you may say all you need to. I do not know what closure you might gain— or even if he will offer any apology, but we shall try. I only ask one thing."

"What is that?"

"That you do not mention the child," Darcy said.

Charles nodded. "Of course not. I would not see that scoundrel lay even his eyes upon her."

"Then we are in agreement," Darcy said.

"Yes. Tomorrow."

* * *

THE DAMP CHILL of the Covent Garden air seemed to cling to Darcy's very bones as he and Bingley stood before the same run down tavern where they had previously found Mr. Jonathan Barry.

The dank odor of spilled ale wafted out through the open door, momentarily making Darcy hesitate before stepping inside. Bingley, ever eager, led the way into the dimly lit establishment.

"Gentlemen," the bartender greeted them with a suspicious smile. "I've only just opened my doors— Eager to have a pint?"

"We are not here for a drink, sir," Darcy replied tersely. "We are searching for Jonathan Darcy. He was the man we spoke with when we were last here."

The bartender's eyes narrowed as he recalled their last visit to his deplorable establishment.

"Aye, I know who he is. A bit worse for wear, he was, after that conversation with you. He stumbled out shortly after. I've not seen him since. Some kind of trouble? I'll not be havin' any of that here."

Darcy exchanged an uneasy glance with Bingley and then turned his attention to the assortment of patrons scattered throughout the room. "No, no," he said to the war bartender. "You'll have no trouble from us."

Darcy stood back as Charles moved through the room and approached the other patrons one by one to inquire about Jonathan. But from the look on his face, none of them had any information to offer. Frustration gnawed at the edges of Darcy's thoughts, but he refused to let it consume him completely.

"Charles," Darcy called out. "We must move on."

They left the tavern and made their way to the boarding house where Jonathan had taken lodging. Charles seemed determined to scour every tavern and house of ill-repute, but Darcy knew it was only a waste of time. However, Charles would not be dissuaded. Darcy accompanied his friend to every tavern on the filthy street, but each time Charles emerged more downcast than before.

Finally, he agreed to visit the boarding house at the end of the lane.

They had no other means of finding Jonathan Barry.

As they entered the boarding house, the same elderly proprietor greeted them at the door.

"Good day again, sirs," she croaked, her voice as creaky as the floorboards beneath their feet. "What brings you back to my humble establishment?"

"Madam," Darcy began with a respectful nod, "we are still looking for Jonathan Darcy—does he rent a room here?"

"Hm..." she mused, rubbing her chin thoughtfully and irritation gnawed at Darcy's gut. "A troubled soul, to be sure."

"Here now," Charles exclaimed. "We were here not three days past and you said—"

Darcy placed a hand on Charles' shoulder and tightened his grip. "Not now," he muttered.

He knew the woman was withholding information, but being angry with her would solve nothing.

Darcy pulled a shiny crown from his pocket and held it out to her. "We would greatly appreciate any information you could provide regarding his whereabouts."

The woman's eyes gleamed with interest as she snatched the coin from Darcy's fingers. "Well, now that you mention it, the constable came by not long after you collected your coats and took him away.... I haven't seen 'im since." Her voice held no warmth or concern; it was clear that she was only interested in what profit could be gained from what she knew.

"Thank you, madam," Darcy replied.

The constable? What could Jonathan have done in the last two days to justify a visit from the authorities?

They had found some answers, but their search was far from over.

"What now?" Charles asked. "I have half a mind to abandon the wretch to his own fate."

"We must find out the truth," Darcy said. "If there is something that can be done, we must try."

"He is your relation," Charles snapped. "Not mine."

Irritated, Darcy grabbed Charles' elbow. "No, he is not. But you will accompany me all the same."

Bingley muttered something Darcy could not hear, but he did not care. Together they trudged through the streets toward the local constabulary.

The stone building was small, but formidable and seemed to cast a strange sort of pallor over the street.

"Let us hope we find good news within," Darcy muttered as he pushed open the door.

The interior of the building was dark and oppressive, lit dimly by flickering lanterns that gave off more smoke than light. A uniformed man sat behind a wooden desk, his quill scratched noisily against rough paper as he recorded some unknown detail of the city's daily chaos. He looked up as they approached, and his eyes narrowed suspiciously at their fine attire.

"Can I help you, gentlemen?" he asked gruffly, clearly unused to such well-dressed visitors.

"I hope you can," Darcy replied. "We are looking for information regarding one Jonathan Darcy—Jonathan Barry is his real name. We have reason to believe he was taken into custody a few days ago."

"Darcy, eh?" the constable muttered as he flipped through the pages of his logbook. His finger finally landed on a line of text, and his grin widened as he read. "Ah yes, here he is. Jonathan Darcy was arrested for housebreaking near Hampstead Heath. Bad business that. He was found guilty this morning—"

"Guilty," Darcy repeated.

"Guilty," the constable confirmed. "Transported."

"To where?" Bingley chimed in.

The constable leaned back in his chair. "Not to anyplace you'd want to go," he said. "He went where all of them go— Van Diemen's Land."

"Went—" Darcy said. "As in, he is already gone?"

The constable nodded. "The ship left this morning."

Darcy felt as if the weight of the world was lifted off of his shoulders. The permanence of Jonathan's fate echoed through his mind.

"I— I have not even heard of that place," Bingley stammered. "For life?"

"And is there any way to appeal the sentence?" Darcy asked, fighting to keep his voice steady.

"None," the constable replied, shaking his head. "Once a man is sent off, there's nothing anyone can do. Who wants a thief in their house?"

Darcy could not think of an intelligent answer to that statement. Instead he stepped away from the man's desk. "Thank you for your assistance," Darcy managed to say. He turned and walked blindly out of the station, and Bingley followed silently until they were clear of the building and out on the cobbled street.

Jonathan was gone, sent halfway around the world to a life of hardship and forced labor in a faraway colony.

And Darcy could not be happier.

Amelia was safe.

"The ladies will be overjoyed with this news," Bingley said. "Although I must say I am dissatisfied that I am not able to put my fist into Jonathan Barry's face on Caroline's behalf."

"There are other matters to take care of," Darcy said as they turned back toward Mayfair. "You and Miss Bennet can continue to plan your wedding, and life can finally go on... for all of us."

They had done all they could to make sure Jonathan would remain gone, and now they needed to focus on protecting those they held dear. It was time to return home and build the lives they planned...

elizabeth

IT WAS from Jane that Elizabeth learned that Mr. Bingley would not lay claim to Amelia.

"I— I would wish that it were different," Jane said tearfully, "but he would not be persuaded. I know the scandal— And Louisa... Charles would not even consider telling her. There would be no recovery from the shame of it. Although, how someone could be ashamed of little Amelia seems impossible to consider."

Elizabeth wrapped her arms around her sister, offering comfort and understanding. "I know it is a difficult decision for Mr. Bingley," she said softly. "And I cannot fault him for it. The potential for scandal and the strain it could place on your marriage, and the effect her presence could have on your position in society, is not something to be taken lightly. But I cannot help but feel a sense of relief that Amelia will remain in Mr. Darcy's care. He has proven himself to be a devoted and loving guardian."

Jane nodded and wiped away a stray tear. "You are right, Lizzy. Mr. Darcy has shown such kindness and compassion toward Amelia. I have no doubt that she will thrive under his care. And with you by his side as her governess— I know very well that she will want for nothing."

Elizabeth felt a flush of warmth at her sister's words. The thought of remaining at Pemberley, of being a constant presence in Amelia's life and in Mr. Darcy's, filled her with a sense of contentment and purpose she had never known before.

"I am grateful for the opportunity to continue in my role," she said, a smile playing at the corners of her mouth. "In such a short time, Amelia has captured my heart, and I cannot imagine being parted from her. And Mr. Darcy... he has proven himself to be a man of great integrity and compassion. I admire him greatly."

Jane's eyes sparkled with understanding. "I do believe, dear sister, that your admiration extends beyond mere respect for his character. I have seen the way you look at him, and the way he looks at you in return... There is a deep affection there, one that has grown through your shared devotion to Amelia."

Elizabeth felt her cheeks grow warm at her sister's astute observation. She could not deny the truth of it—her feelings for Mr. Darcy had indeed blossomed into something far deeper than she had ever anticipated. His kindness, his commitment to Amelia's well-being, and the quiet strength of his character had all served to endear him to her in ways she was only beginning to understand.

"I... I cannot deny that my regard for Mr. Darcy has grown," she admitted softly, her gaze flitting to the window where the sun was beginning to set over the rooftops of London. "But Jane, I dare not hope for more. He is a man of great wealth and consequence, and I am— Well, at the moment I am but a humble governess. Surely he could not see me as anything more than a caretaker for his ward."

Jane reached out and grasped Elizabeth's hands. "Do not underestimate your own worth, Lizzy. *Any* man would be fortunate to have you by his side, regardless of wealth or status. And from what I have observed, Mr. Darcy values you for far more than your role as Amelia's governess. He respects your opinions, he seeks out your counsel, and I can see that he finds great comfort in your presence."

Elizabeth felt a flicker of hope ignite in her chest at her sister's words.

Could it be true?

Could Mr. Darcy harbor feelings for her that went beyond gratitude or friendship?

The thought both thrilled and terrified her.

"I... I hardly dare to hope, Jane," she whispered. "But I cannot deny that the thought of a future with Mr. Darcy, and of raising Amelia together and building a life at Pemberley, fills me with... I cannot even find the words to explain it. Do you truly think it possible that he could come to see me as more than a governess?"

Jane smiled, her expression warm and reassuring. "I do, Lizzy. I have seen the way his gaze lingers on you when you are not looking—his stoic expression only breaks when you enter the room. And the care and tenderness with which he treats Amelia speaks to the kind of husband, and father, he would be. I do believe it."

Elizabeth's heart fluttered at Jane's words. Could she truly allow herself to dream of a future with Mr. Darcy, one in which they raised Amelia together as a family? The very thought filled her with a warmth and longing she had never experienced before.

The very deepest love—something she had thought would never be hers.

Perhaps it could.

"Oh Jane," Elizabeth sighed, leaning her head against her sister's shoulder. "I want to believe it possible. But I fear allowing my heart to hope, only to have those hopes dashed... Mr. Darcy is a proud man, and rightfully so given his station. Even if he does harbor some affection for me, would he truly consider marrying so far beneath him?"

Before Jane could answer that question, Mrs. Gardiner swept into the room.

"Lizzy— Mr. Darcy's carriage has arrived to carry you and Miss Amelia back to Pemberley. Are you ready to depart?"

Elizabeth's heart leapt into her throat at her aunt's words.

So soon?

She had thought there would be more time, more opportunity to sort through the tumult of emotions swirling within her. But it seemed fate had other plans.

She rose from her seat and smoothed her skirts with trembling hands. "I... yes, of course. Amelia and I shall be ready to depart shortly." She turned to her sister. "Oh Jane, what if—"

Jane silenced her with a smile. "Do not borrow trouble, Lizzy. Go to Pemberley with an open heart and mind. Allow yourself to hope, and to dream. I have a feeling that your future may be brighter than you dare to imagine."

Elizabeth drew in a shaky breath and nodded, drawing strength from her sister's unwavering support. "You are right, as always. I shall try to keep my doubts at bay just as you have."

With that, she embraced Jane tightly, whispering her love and gratitude before hurrying to collect little Amelia and their belongings.

As she settled into the plush carriage with Amelia cradled securely in her arms, Elizabeth felt a flutter of anticipation and nerves.

Everything would change yet again—

As the cityscape faded into countryside, Elizabeth breathed a sigh of relief. The Derbyshire landscape rolled by, and with each passing mile, Elizabeth felt herself drawing closer not only to Pemberley, but to the man who had come to mean so much to her.

Mr. Fitzwilliam Darcy.

The very thought of his name sent a thrill through her veins.

Over these past weeks—no, it had been more than two months now, she had seen a side of him that few others were privileged to witness. He was a devoted guardian, a compassionate friend, and a man of unwavering integrity. And with each passing day, her admiration and affection for him had grown and blossomed into something far deeper and more meaningful than she had ever dared to dream possible.

As the carriage wound its way down the tree-lined drive leading to the grand estate, Elizabeth's heart raced.

She cradled a sleeping Amelia close and drew comfort from the baby's soft warmth and steady breathing.

The carriage rolled to a stop before the imposing front entrance of Pemberley and Elizabeth waited for the footman to open the door before she alighted carefully, Amelia still nestled securely in her arms.

As she crossed the courtyard and ascended the stone steps, her legs felt strangely unsteady beneath her. As she reached the top, the great oaken door swung open, revealing the tall, handsome figure of Mr. Darcy himself.

"You are most welcome home," he said warmly.

Elizabeth had expected him to be dressed more formally, as he had been in London, but now that he was back at Pemberley, all pretense had been forgotten and he was dressed in a rough linen shirt and breeches that were spattered with mud.

Elizabeth smiled up at him. "I see you have been at the farms again," she said.

"I have," he admitted. "Would you like to see them?"

Elizabeth shifted Amelia slightly in her arms. "I would. As

soon as I can put Amelia into her cradle. I am certain she is exhausted from her journey—"

Darcy chuckled and stepped forward to take the child gently from her arms. "I cannot argue with you," he said. "She seems entirely overwrought."

"But I would welcome a walk," Elizabeth said. "Being trapped in a carriage for long distances certainly requires some exercise at its end."

Darcy smiled warmly as he cradled the sleeping Amelia in his strong arms. "Of course. A walk sounds most agreeable after your long journey. Allow me to settle Amelia in the nursery—I know Mrs. Reynolds is eager to welcome her back into the household. I shall return presently to escort you."

Elizabeth felt a strange flutter in her chest as she Darcy disappeared into the house with Amelia, his gentle care and devotion to the child evident in every movement. She took a moment to compose herself and smoothed her travel-rumpled skirts and re-tied the strings of her bonnet.

Within moments, Darcy returned, a soft smile gracing his handsome features. "Shall we?" he asked, offering his arm to her.

Elizabeth took his proffered arm and together, they stepped out into the lush gardens of Pemberley.

As they strolled along the winding path, Elizabeth found herself drawn into easy conversation with Darcy. He spoke of the improvements he had made to the tenant farms since his return, his plans for further renovations to the estate, and his joy at having Amelia under his care and protection. Elizabeth listened attentively, offering her own insights and observations, and delighted in the way Darcy seemed to truly value her opinions.

Perhaps Jane was right—

"Elizabeth, there is something I must ask you," Darcy began

and Elizabeth tried to ignore the thrill that traveled up her spine at his use of her name...

"Of course, Mr. Darcy. What is it that you wish to ask me?" She hoped that he could not hear the tremor in her voice—but it was loud in her own ears.

"Ever since I discovered Amelia and took her into my care, my life has been transformed," he confessed, his gaze never leaving hers. "With you by my side, we have overcome so much —and through it all... you have been unwavering in your devotion to Amelia. And this family."

With each word, Elizabeth's eyes widened, her breath held.

Darcy continued as though he could not stop himself. "Your love for Amelia has inspired me, and your support has given me strength. I... I cannot imagine facing the future without you." He paused, but only for a moment and Elizabeth bit down hard on her lip as he grabbed her hands and held them gently in his.

"Elizabeth Bennet," he said in a rush, "will you do me the honor of... Will you become the mistress of this estate... Will you say that you will be my wife?"

For an instant, time seemed to stand still, as Elizabeth stared at him—filled to the brim with shock. Her eyes stung with unshed tears—tears of happiness—as she nodded assent.

"Mr. Darcy— Fitzwilliam," she choked out. "I— I do not know what to say."

"Say... say what is in your heart," he said. "That is what my own sister would say to me. And it is how I was able to speak just now... I thought I could not do it. I labored for days—"

"I will," Elizabeth blurted out.

Darcy's eyes widened, his expression caught between disbelief and joy. "You... you will? Truly?"

"Yes," Elizabeth breathed, her heart soaring. "Yes, Fitzwilliam, I will marry you. Nothing would make me happier than to be your wife and to raise Amelia together—as a family."

A brilliant smile spread across Darcy's face as he drew Elizabeth into his arms and held her close. "My dearest, loveliest Elizabeth," he murmured against her hair. "You have made me the happiest of men. I promise to love and cherish you all the days of my life."

Tears of joy prickled at the corners of her eyes as she clung to him and basked in the warmth of his embrace. "And I shall love you with all my heart, now and always," she said.

They remained locked in each other's arms for a long moment, savoring the joy and promise of their newly declared love. When at last they parted, Darcy took Elizabeth's hand in his and raised it to his lips to press a tender kiss to her knuckles.

"Come, my love," he said softly. "Let us return to the house and share our joyous news with Mrs. Reynolds and the staff. I am certain they will be overjoyed to learn that their beloved Miss Bennet is to become the new mistress of Pemberley."

Elizabeth laughed, her heart light and free.

"I can think of nothing better," she said. "But first, will you take me to see the tenant farms?"

Darcy's smile was broad and sunny. "Mrs. Reynolds will scold us for our muddy feet," he cautioned.

"Let her," Elizabeth declared. "You may be afraid of her stern words, but I am not. Lead the way, sir!"

THE END

more from blue flowers press